# ABOUT THE AUTHOR

Dr. David Reid was born in Greenock in 1947. He has lived with his wife in Dunfermline for over 40 years. After graduating from Edinburgh University in Civil Engineering in 1969, he worked for Lothian regional council, designing bridges before moving into teaching. He lectured in applied mathematics for engineering students, initially at Kirkcaldy College, then Edinburgh Napier University and latterly at Anglia Ruskin University, where he was Head of Department and finally Deputy Dean of the Faculty of Science. Now retired he still tutors mathematics with the Open University in Edinburgh which he has done since 1986.

to Dawn and Roy
hope you enjoy the read
you will recognise many
of the locations that
I've used
David

David 15/12/21

# THE

# SPANISH

# STATUETTE

DAVID BOWMAN REID

Matador
9 Priory Business Park,
Wistow Road, Kibworth Beauchamp,
Leicestershire. LE8 0RX
Tel: 0116 279 2299
Email: books@troubador.co.uk
Web: www.troubador.co.uk/matador
Twitter: @matadorbooks

ISBN 978 1800463 981

British Library Cataloguing in Publication Data.
A catalogue record for this book is available from the British Library.

Typeset in 11pt Minion Pro by Troubador Publishing Ltd, Leicester, UK

Matador is an imprint of Troubador Publishing Ltd

To my wife, Sheila, and my family who have helped and encouraged me to complete this book; also, to our friends, remembering the many happy holidays that we have spent together in Spain and will do again in the future.

# CONTENTS

# PROLOGUE

The Dama de Baza (Lady of Baza) statue was found inside an underground chamber during the excavation of tomb 155 of the Necropolis del Santuario outside the town of Baza in Granada province, Spain on the 21$^{st}$ July 1971. It revealed a great deal about the artistic environment and burial world of the ancient Iberians.

The statue depicts the figure of a woman on a throne and is sculptured from a single stone block of sandstone painted in red, blue white and black. The robes and adornments indicate a woman of high social status and is similar to other representations of Mediterranean goddesses.

The original 135cm high statue is now in the Museo Arqueologica Nacional in Madrid but a replica is to be found in the local museum in Baza. Ornamental miniature versions are on sale in many shops in the town.

# AUTHOR'S NOTE

*This is a work of fiction. Although the locations are real, all the characters, businesses, events and incidents in this book are either the product of the author's imagination or used in a fictitious manner. Any resemblance to actual persons, living or dead, or actual events is purely coincidental.*

# 1

## WAITING

*"Alea iacta est." "The die is cast."*

La Solana was an unremarkable cafe, with nothing of note to mark it out from scores of others in Granada. But it served its purpose as the meeting place in the evenings for those who lived nearby. Only a few visitors to the city ever found their way to La Solana which was in a narrow lane in the maze of tapered streets between Calle de San Jeronimo and the cathedral. Those who did would come across it by chance rather than design, giving it only a cursory glance before passing it by.

It was late August, and although it was past 10 in the evening, the temperature was still above 25°C. The lane was dark and deserted. Inside La Solana the obligatory television was showing some chat show on the tiny screen high up on a ledge in the far corner of the cramped, dimly lit bar. As usual, no one appeared to be interested or paid it much attention. The majority of the clientele, some dozen or so, were regulars and fully engrossed in their own conversations. Most sat at the bar, but others occupied a few of the old, worn, wooden tables which were haphazardly arranged over the litter strewn floor. The tables were covered in empty glasses and plates. The barman, a thin, dark haired youth in his early twenties, showed little enthusiasm to clear these away, being more interested in adding his views to the talk of the previous weekend Seville v Barcelona football match. The smell of stale cigarette smoke and unfinished tapas filled the room and seemed to cling to the scored green walls. Cheap, faded prints of the city and bullfight posters randomly clung to the walls, the curled edges betraying the passage of time. The single small window by the entrance door offered the only view out into the lane and this was masked by a stained net curtain which hung limply from hooks in the wall. On a narrow shelf below the window were an array of cheap, dust covered ornaments; a tiny black bull, two shabby, faded fans, a pair of wooden castanets that had seen better days, and a small statuette depicting the Dama de Baza.

The two men sitting at the table near the window were alone. Both were in their mid-forties. The taller of the two wore a smart, well cut suit. He was slim, with a taught sun-tanned face, dark, intense eyes and well-groomed black hair. He gave off the self-assured air of a successful businessman. His companion looked more nervous, consulting his watch and frequently looking over towards the entrance door. This second man was heavier built with a paler complexion and looked as if he hadn't shaved for a few days. He wore a baggy, threadbare cardigan over a pair of jeans. "When will we know for sure, Carlos? This waiting is getting to me; it's been over a week now since we last heard anything."

"Be patient José. Hernandez will be in touch when things are in place and it's time. For now, relax."

José walked over to the bar and passed the waiter a five-euro note. The bar man took it went to the till and returned with five one-euro coins. Nothing had needed to be said. This was obviously a frequent process. José took the coins and went over to the brightly coloured flashing fruit machine in the corner. He put the first coin into the machine and pulled the handle, the dials span; orange, lemon, cherry, orange. Nothing. He pulled the handle again; strawberry, lemon, lemon orange. Nothing. Carlos shouted across to him, "Leave it José. These machines have pre-set odds and are designed to take your money. You can't win and you are spending faster than we are earning!"

José pulled the handle again; orange, orange, cherry, lemon. Nothing. He inserted a second coin; bar, bar, strawberry, bar. A note flashed on the edge of the screen, Two Nudges. José pressed the nudge on the third disc. The display changed to lemon. He pressed the same nudge again and it changed to cherry. Just above the cherry, but not in the pay-out line, he could see a bar. José banged the machine with his fist in frustration.

# 2

## A RUDE AWAKENING

"Could I have your attention please? Would Dr. Crawford please make himself known to one of the cabin crew, thank you?"

Sam Crawford was only faintly aware of the announcement over the aircraft intercom as he dozed, uncomfortably in his cramped seat. "Sam, Sam, that call is for you." Sam Crawford's sister, Helen, was sitting beside him and had been distracted from the book she was reading by this unexpected development. She gently, but firmly, nudged her brother with her elbow into his side. "Sam, are you awake?"

The Boeing 737 was now about two hours into its flight from Manchester to Almeria in southern Spain. From the small windows it would have been impossible for any passenger, sufficiently interested, to be precisely certain as to where they now were. All that could be seen through the breaks in the clouds were brown coloured rectangular blocks of fields surrounded by low stonewalls with the occasional road or track breaking up the monotony of the barren landscape.

"Sam. Wake up, will you." Sam stirred and slowly became more aware of his surroundings. "That call just now on the intercom, it was for you!"

"Why would it be for me?"

"I don't know do I. Don't you think you had better press the call button and find out?"

Sam gazed around the inside of the plane. He was sitting in the centre seat of three. On his right, at the window, was his sister Helen, while on his left, in the aisle seat, was a rather large woman. Sam estimated that the woman was probably in her early forties but they had hardly acknowledged each other since taking their seats. She had seemed content with her personal music which she listened to through a set of earphones. Her eyes were firmly closed and the beat of the tunes filtered out into the cabin. It was only just audible to Sam. The tune was muffled and indiscernible. Most of the other passengers were either reading or dozing. Three rows ahead a young couple were attempting to keep their two young children amused with colouring books and a seemingly endless supply of sweets. At the front of the plane there was the inevitable queue for the toilets.

"For goodness sake press the call button," said Helen with more than a little impatience in her voice. Reluctantly

Sam raised his arm to the button above his seat and pressed it firmly. It made a pleasantly tuneful boing and the light beside it lit up. "I don't think they mean me", protested Sam.

"Course they do", insisted Helen. "How many Dr. Crawfords do you think there are on this plane?"

The stewardess appeared at the end of the row of seats. She looked anxious and a little flustered. "Dr. Crawford, thank goodness you are on board. We have a minor emergency at the rear of the plane. One of the passengers has taken unwell. Nothing serious, I think. Bit of flight sickness. But we do need some medical help. I checked the passenger list and noticed your name. Could you come with me quickly, please!" And with that she set off back down the plane.

Sam looked across at his sister. She had a large wide grin across her face. "You best go and explain," said Helen, "It sounds as if some poor soul could do with some assistance. Pity you won't be much use to them". The smile broadened on her face. Helen was nine years younger than Sam and they had been close since children.

Reluctantly Sam unbuckled his seat belt and stood up as straight as possible in the cramped confines between his seat and the row in front. His sharp movement alerted the large woman who was blocking his exit to the centre aisle. Grudgingly she squeezed her way up and out into the passageway to make way for Sam, treading on the toes of a young boy who happened to be passing by just at that moment. The youngster let out a squeal of intense pain and ran off up the plane towards his parents. "I'm sorry about this," offered Sam feeling the apology rather inadequate in the circumstances. Once out into the isle Sam could see clearly down the passageway towards the tail end of the aircraft. The stewardess, some thirty feet or so away, was beckoning him to hurry and, somewhat unsteadily, Sam gradually made his way swaying from side to side. The manoeuvre seemed to be particularly difficult. The plane was flying through a spot of turbulence exaggerating Sam's staggering movements. Eventually, through a process of two steps forward and one back, Sam arrived at the spot occupied by the stewardess. She was standing alongside a seat occupied by a young man sporting a football shirt, track suit bottoms and an extremely grey complexion. He was obviously in some discomfort and certainly not enjoying his experience of flying. His travelling companion, similarly attired but with an allegiance to another club, seemed somewhat disinterested in his friend's problem. Both appeared to be suffering from a little over indulgence in early morning airport lager, probably accentuated by the two-hour delay in take-off from Manchester. Having weighed up the situation Sam was, to say the least, more than a little relieved. "Can you do anything for him Dr. Crawford?" asked the stewardess rather hopefully. "He has been terribly sick since I came around with the scrambled eggs and bacon breakfast. He looks so miserable and we have another hour before we land at Almeria."

"Not much. I don't cope very well with people who are ill. Makes me panicky. Can't stand the sight of blood and all that sort of thing. Makes me feel faint. I'm best kept well out of the way in any emergency".

"What! I don't understand? But you are a ..."

"My doctorate is in mathematics not medicine. I just came back to explain to you."

Sam watched the look of disdain grow on her face. "Sorry." It was time, he felt, to retreat up the aisle to leave the cabin crew to deal with things as best they could. Helen watched as he settled back down into his seat. "You weren't long. A miracle cure was it?"

"Very funny. Fortunately, it's no more than a bit of over indulgence. When are we due to land? I hate being cooped up like this. I swear that they shove more seats into these things each year. My knees are hard against that seat in front. Either that or I'm still growing at 54. Do you think the man in front needs to have his seat in the recline position throughout the whole flight? I swear that during the meal I had to drop the food into my mouth from vertically above."

"For goodness sake try and relax. We will be beginning the decent shortly. Check the details for the hire car that we are picking up or something to pass the time. Why don't you read more of the book that you brought with you?"

"I've given up on it. The plot is far-fetched and the coincidences are improbable. Real life is not like that."

"It's just escapism for goodness sake. Chill out!"

The remainder of the flight was uneventful and Sam spent the time running over in his mind the events that had led up to him now being aboard this flight to the eastern end of the Costa del Sol. Strictly Mojacar is not on the Costa del Sol. It's about a one-hour drive north from Almeria airport via the road through Carboneras, nestling at the foot of the Sierra Cabrera at the point where the mountains reach the Mediterranean coast line. The acceptance of the offer of an early retirement package from the university had been an easy decision for Sam to make. After all he didn't need the money now. His two girls were now adults and self-sufficient. A second mortgage on the house in Edinburgh had been easy to obtain. Prices had gone through the roof since he and Carol first bought it in the early 1980s and with that and a bit of the retirement package Sam had been able to purchase a neat little villa in Mojacar Playa. Sam's intention was to occupy it for about three months of the year in early summer and to rent it out through a letting agency for as much of the rest of the year as demand would permit, allowing some time for use by the girls and various close friends.

The choice of Mojacar had been an easy one to make. The Crawfords had spent many holidays in Spain when the girls were growing up and one way and another, they had explored most of the coast line from Barcelona to Gibraltar. By a process of elimination Sam had been able to whittle down his favoured areas until finally selecting Mojacar basically for two reasons; firstly, because he loved the atmosphere of the old town, Mojacar Pueblo, and secondly due to the relative proximity of his favourite Spanish city, Granada. Mojacar Playa, where he had bought the villa is about 2 kilometres from the Pueblo and consists more or less of a single road, the Paseo del Mediterraneo, which winds its way along the sandy beach. Few of the buildings rise above two stories and the tiny streets, or more accurately tracks, which lead back from the Paseo del Mediterraneo are bordered by seemingly randomly placed white villas. On one such track Sam had found the Villa Campomar.

Villa Campomar fitted his needs perfectly and he had fallen in love with the place when shown over the property for the first time by the selling agent. The house was modest in size comprising of two compact bedrooms, one with its own small balcony, a comfortable living room which opened out onto a further larger balcony with views down to the neat front courtyard, a kitchen and bathroom and an external staircase which led to the roof terrace. From the roof terrace, looking northward you could see the road winding its way up the hillside towards the old town. Looking southward you could see over the roofs of the various randomly scattered villas to the coast line and the small central area of the Playa. During the summer months, the roof terrace would be bathed in Mediterranean sunshine from early morning till evening. The community, of which Villa Campomar formed part, consisted of some twelve similar properties. They shared a secluded garden area with a communal pool which was surrounded by various fruit trees and trestles sporting deep purple and pink bougainvillea.

Renting out during June and July had been no problem. The lets had been arranged through the local agents, Indalo Properties, who had seen to all the booking details, the cleaning and laundry and the general enquiries and needs of the holiday makers staying their week or two weeks in the villa. It was now the first week in August and

Sam had set aside the next four weeks for himself. The agent had advised that this was still prime rental period but, after all, he had bought the place for his own pleasure. The bookings had already exceeded expectations and would more than cover the running costs and various community charges so the next four weeks were for Sam to relax in and unwind. The only commitment was the guest lecture that he had promised to give on the last Friday in August at the University of Granada. This wouldn't prove too much of a chore and besides the university had paid for, and arranged the flights for him as recompense.

Sam looked expectantly out of the window of the plane. It was now a full three years since the unexplained disappearance of his wife, Carol, during a weekend holiday break in Florence. The intercom sprang into life again. "We are about to begin our descent towards Almeria. Would all passengers please return to their seats and fasten their seatbelts. The local time is 3.30. The weather is dry and sunny with a current temperature at the airport of 32 degrees."

"Yes, perhaps this is just what I need," thought Sam.

Once the plane had landed and taxied its way to the terminal building there was the usual delay before the doors opened. Sam got out of his seat and retrieved the hand luggage from the overhead locker. Eventually the stream of passengers began to exit and make their way down the steps at the rear exit. Sam and Helen stepped out into the bright sunshine and warm air making them both smile. It didn't take long to clear passport control and to collect their suitcases from the carousel. They walked through to the arrivals floor, passing the assembly of families and tour representatives standing behind the low barriers, who were eagerly observing the stream of passengers as they passed by. Sam and Helen paid little attention to them as they made their way to the car hire desks and certainly did not see the man standing discretely in the second row. He was on his phone. In a low voice he said, "He's arrived."

# 3

## VILLA CAMPOMAR

Villa Campomar was very much as Sam remembered it. It was quite some time since his last visit. He had never really had the enthusiasm to return now that Carol was not with him. It had taken a considerable amount of gentle persuasion and effort on Helen's part to even get him to think about the possibility of again spending some time there.

"You need the break". "You have to get over the past and move on", she had reasoned and slowly, bit by bit Sam had come around to accepting the truth in what she was saying.

Still, it seemed strange and unreal to be standing at the front door. Doubts about the wisdom of returning filled his mind and he was uncertain that he would have courage to enter. His mind was filled with images of how things had been; the warm summer mornings, when the two of them would take breakfast on the terrace, sheltered from the sun's rays by the awning that Sam had bought from the market in Almeria, the lazy afternoons by the communal pool and the peaceful evenings eating good food and sipping fine wine, Sam with a glass of Rioja, Faustino 1 if the funds allowed, and Carol with her red wine mixed with casera or tinto de verano as the locals called it.

Sam swung the door open and stepped inside. The door led directly into the living room. Sam's shoes clacked on the titled floor. Looking around his eyes fell on the various ornaments that decorated the shelves in the alcoves on the far wall, small items of little value that would easily escape one's notice. But each item encapsulated a memory for Sam; each brought back thoughts of how things had been; the Don Quixote ornament bought during a weekend trip to Toledo, the framed prints on the walls from Antequera, the tiny statuette of the Dama de Baza set in the alcove, and on the floor, the hand-woven carpets from Lanjaron and Pampaneira high in the Alpujarra.

Helen watched Sam's eyes as they slowly took in the scene, fully aware of the thoughts that must have been going through his head. "Move over Samuel, you're blocking the doorway."

"I'm not sure that this was such a good idea."

"Look Sam you have to confront these issues if you are ever to make a new life for yourself. You need to get yourself back on track; find new interests to occupy your time."

"You are right of course, but I don't think that this might be the best place to do that."

Next morning sitting on the terrace with the sun beating down Sam's thoughts turned to the events in Italy three years earlier. He had been over this so many times in his mind before. What had exactly happened on that fateful day in Florence when he and Carol had gone out from the hotel on the Via Della Scala? It seemed such an ordinary day. They had been in Florence for four days visiting the usual tourist sites: the Pitti Palace, the Basillica Santa Croce, the Bargello sculpture gallery and the Duomo. That day it was to be the turn of the Uffizi with its countless Renaissance and Baroque paintings: Giotto, Bottecelli, Leonardo da Vinci, Michelangelo, Raphael, Caravaggio and others. To be honest Sam had just about had his fill of culture. This was more Carol's thing. She had always been the more artistic of the partnership. Sam was happier with the practicalities of science and mathematics. The tickets that they had pre-booked for the Uffizi had a tour start time of 1pm. It was just after 11.00am so there was plenty of time for a coffee in one of the cafes in the Plaza Della Signoria, a two-minute walk from the main entrance. Over coffee Carol had flicked through the guide book with enthusiasm jotting down the "must-sees" while at the same time planning a route to ensure that none of these were missed. "Sam, Bottecelli's Birth of Venus is a must, as is Leonardo's Annunciation, then there is Caravaggio's Bucchus and …" Sam had looked across the table at his wife. It was clear from the expression on her face that this was to be the highlight of the trip for her. "Carol, I really think that you should do this particular visit on your own," Sam had ventured trying hard not to sound too disparaging, nor to dampen Carol's enthusiasm. "You know what I am like in art galleries. I get bored and move you through the paintings quicker than you would do if you were on your own. I have enjoyed the galleries that we have visited over the past four days but I think that I have had enough culture for one short trip. I would honestly be quite happy to wander around some bookshops while you view the masterpieces of the Uffizi at your own pace." Sam had looked carefully at Carol to see the effect of his suggestion, unsure that he may have disappointed her. On the contrary, a broad smile had passed over her face.

"Sure Sam. I agree with you. I was going to suggest the same thing but I was afraid that you might think me selfish. It's not that I don't want you to come but these paintings need time to be fully appreciated. A quick glance, then on to the next is insufficient. Besides I know that you will be happy browsing through the bookshops and we can arrange a time to meet up here in the café and then go for meal in that restaurant near the Pitti Palace that we like so much. Book a table for 7pm and I will meet you back here at 6.30. We can walk to the restaurant and fill each other in regards our separate afternoons."

And so it was agreed. Carol had finished her coffee, waving to Sam as she went out into the Plaza heading towards the short queue that had formed with those having pre-booked for 1pm.

"Sam, here's the cool beer that I promised to bring out to you." Helen jogged Sam back into the present. "I would have brought it out here on the terrace earlier but you looked as if you were asleep and I didn't want to disturb you."

————————

"José…José! Get over here! I have just had a message from Hernandez. Our contact arrived at Almeria yesterday. His flight from Manchester was delayed by 2 hours. We are to wait here for further instructions."

# 4

## BAZA REMEMBERED

It was approaching mid-day and by now the heat was unbearable, even under the shade of the large red and yellow sun shade and Sam decided it was time to go indoors. Inside the villa Helen was deeply engrossed in the book that she had bought at Manchester airport. She raised her eyes as Sam came into the living room.

"Are you alright Sam?"

"Yes, fine. It's just a little too hot to sit out there at the moment." The aircon system was a good twenty years old and rattled a bit but the room was relatively comfortable. "You go on reading. I think I'll lie down for a bit. The heat is exhausting even when you are doing nothing. The Spanish have the right idea with their siestas." Helen's attention returned to her book and Sam walked towards the rear bedroom casually picking up the small Dama de Baza statuette on the way. He placed the statuette on the desk in the corner of the room, took off his shoes and lay down on the bed on top of the duvet. The statuette had always been one of his favourite pieces that he and Carol had bought from the little store in the Plaza Major in Baza many years before.

Stopping in Baza had not been part of the original plan for the Seville trip. They had turned off the motorway looking for somewhere to have a coffee stop and perhaps some tapas. Baza had proved to be a good choice. The neat town was well served with shops and restaurants and both he and Carol were immediately taken by the clean, narrow streets leading to the centre of the town.

Parking had been easy and they walked into the Plaza Major. The plaza was wide and traffic free. Children were laughing and running around the fountain. The scene was dominated by the stone-built cathedral. On the opposite side of the plaza from the cathedral were a collection of small shops, a chemist and a restaurant. Outside the restaurant were a cluster of tables occupied by locals enjoying cool refreshing drinks. The whole atmosphere of the place was friendly and inviting. They had sat down at a free table and ordered an orange juice and a beer.

"Un zumo de naranja y una cerveza. Gracias."

"Algo mas?" asked the waitress.

"Nada mas", confirmed Sam.

The drinks arrived promptly accompanied by a small plate of tapas and two forks. While Sam and Carol sat and ate, they gazed around the plaza. It was almost a perfect square in shape with tall buildings on all four sides. Narrow alleyways led off at various points on each of the sides, the one to the left of the cathedral was where they had come in. Next to the restaurant was a two-story museum building with a tourist information desk visible just inside the open doors.

Sam could still picture the location perfectly but he couldn't remember whose suggestion it was to abandon the trip to Seville and instead spend a few days in Baza before returning to the coast and was it decided while they sat at the table or latter after their visit to the museum? It didn't matter. They had both agreed.

The bill paid, they had entered the museum and approached the tourist information desk. Sam remembered thinking that this would be a stiffer test of his Spanish. Ok he could order meals and drinks competently but at the coast there was little call to do more as everyone including the Spanish could speak English. Actually, most of the Spanish there could also speak German, Italian and a little French besides. Here, away from the coast, it would be unreasonable to expect the assistant to speak English. Anyway, Sam reasoned he could do with the practice.

However, after Sam's opening remark, "Habla Ingles?" it became quite evident that the assistant behind the desk could speak a very passable version of English, certainly much superior to Sam's Spanish. "How can I help you?" she smiled. Her dark eyes sparkled in the friendly way that Sam had found in most of his encounters with the

Spanish. She had jet black hair which shone in the light streaming into the small office from the window high up in the wall behind her. She was dressed in a smart uniform and in front of her were a collection of leaflets and maps neatly presented in piles on the desk.

"My wife and I intend to spend a few days in the area and I wondered if you could suggest where we might stay and what we should visit when we are here" he explained.

"Bueno. Here we have "Como si dece en Ingles?" leaflets on Baza and a list of our hotels and prices. Baza is rich in history and you must visit el Palacio de Los Enriques, los Banos Arabes, la Iglasia Mayor-Colegiatta, el Monistario de San Jeronimo amongst others, if you have the time. But I suggest that you start by looking around the museum upstairs where we have a full-size replica of La Dama de Baza. The original was moved to Madrid some time ago. It is an example of an early Iberian limestone sculpture. The sculpture was uncovered in 1971 during excavations just outside the town and dates back to the fourth century BC. You take this map of the town. It shows where you will find all these places and where to find the best hotels."

Sam could clearly remember climbing the staircase to the first floor. He had been a few steps ahead of Carol entering the dimly lit exhibition room. On three of the four sides were glass cases containing various artefacts. The long wall opposite the entrance was broken by three large windows which looked out on to the Plaza. In front of the middle window was the sculpture that they had climbed the stairs to see. The impressive life size figure was clearly that of a woman sitting impassively in a wide wing shaped chair. She was richly dressed in a full-length robe. Weighty ear ornaments hung below her simple rounded headdress. Her neck and chest were adorned with heavily carved jewellery. She had a distinctly matriarchal appearance while her face portrayed a certain but unexplained sadness.

On leaving the museum they had crossed the plaza and in one of the small shops bought the small replica of the statuette that was now on the desk opposite Sam. There had been a vast selection to choose from, large and small, various shades of colour. The final choice was made by Carol. The face on that particular model, with its delicate mouth and dark staring eyes, appealed to her. Carol commented that the eyes seemed to transfix you in their gaze, demanding your attention. The impenetrable sadness of the original had been captured effectively. It had been an impulse buy at the time, but something that they later both cherished and came to symbolise and remind them of their time in Baza.

A sharp knock on the bedroom door brought Sam's thoughts back to the present. "Are you awake Sam? You have been asleep in there for hours." Helen's voice sounded from the other side. "I think we should go out for a bit and get some fresh air. It's a bit cooler now and besides it's time we thought about having something to eat." Sam sat up and crossed the room lifting the small ornament as he passed by. In the living room he noticed that the book that Helen had been reading lay closed on the table with the bookmark on top. She had obviously finished it and was now at a loose end.

"Helen, I think that I would like to visit Baza again. On my own if you don't mind. I may set off tomorrow."

———————

"So José, we are to meet Hernandez tomorrow at the finca half way up the road that leads from the village of Zucar to the top of the mountain that they call Jabalcon. You remember Jabalcon. It's about three kilometres outside of Baza."

# 5

---

## TIME TO REFLECT

---

There are two possible routes from Mojacar to Baza. One is by motorway via Puerto Lombreras and Velez Rubio and the other, a more direct but slower road by Albox. Either way the journey would take about two hours. It had just turned 9am when Sam headed out from the coast passing Garrucha and Vera before joining the main road. He could delay his choice of route until the junction at Huercal where the Albox road turned off to the west.

Traffic on the motorway was heavier than he had expected so on reaching the junction he took the slip road and headed towards Albox.

With the sun now at his back and the road substantially quieter Sam was able to relax a bit. Sam had filled the tank of the bright red Seat Ibiza hire car the evening before and he had taken the precaution of bringing a bottle of cold water from the apartment fridge with him. There would be no need to stop on the way to Baza. Sam gazed at the rolling landscape. The sun scorched fields seemed to stretch on for miles on both sides empty except for the occasional finca. In the distance he could see wind-farms high up on the sides of the mountains. The blades of the windmills rotated relentlessly although at road level there was no evidence of even the slightest breath of wind.

As he drove on Sam's thoughts again returned to that fatal day in Florence. He had waved goodbye to Carol as she left the café and headed towards the Uffizi. There was no need for him to rush, there was plenty of time before they were due to meet up again. He finished off his coffee, paid the bill and went out into the Plaza. Sam remembered feeling relieved that Carol had taken his suggestion of spending the afternoon separately so well. He had no real plan, only a general idea that he would visit a few bookshops and pour over their English sections. For what seemed like about an hour he had walked about fairly aimlessly casually looking in shop windows. He even passed by the Uffizi but there was no sign of a queue and he presumed that Carol was already inside with the rest of the 1pm group. Sometime around 1.30pm Sam had entered a bookshop on the Via del Corso.

Time had passed quickly in the bookshop. In the middle of the floor were a number of comfortable seats and couches arranged so that the customers could scan the books that they were considering buying. Sam had taken full advantage of this and had checked out six or seven possible titles before making a choice. Sam had glanced at his watch on leaving the shop. It was still only 3.30pm so there was still three hours before he was due to meet Carol again. He could spend the time by crossing over the river to make the booking at the restaurant as they had arranged.

Sam knew the way well enough; down the lane by the Uffizi, turn right along the banks of the Arno and then left over the Ponte Vecchio. A fresh queue had formed at the Uffizi as he passed by and he had glanced up at the top floor wondering where Carol would be. During the short walk along the edge of the Arno Sam had stopped at a point where several artists were selling cheap print copies of various masterpieces. He spent time looking at these without feeling any desire to buy. Shortly he had arrived at the bridge. Small expensive shops clung to the sides of the Ponte Vecchio and Sam had casually glanced into the windows of some of these as he crossed the river, he was in no hurry.

The restaurant was in a small plaza near the Pitti Palace. Sam and Carol had dined there the previous evening. The waiter recognised Sam immediately. "I am glad you have returned. Yes, a table for two at 7pm is fine. Your wife is not with you just now?" he had said pulling his thick eyebrows together until they almost met to add effect to the question. Sam explained and a broad understanding smile broke out across his face.

The car in front of Sam made a sudden unannounced turn off into a side road on the right forcing Sam to break hard. The automatic action broke Sam's thoughts and he swiftly returned his full attention to his driving. Ahead a worn road sign displayed the message "Caniles 5km, Baza 10km."

In Mojacar Helen decided it was time that she went out. Sitting alone in the villa she found herself worrying about her brother. She reasoned that there was no point in being anxious on his behalf. It was achieving nothing. What had she to be concerned about? Sam spoke less of Carol now and had seemed to have finally accepted that he had to continue his life without her. But why had he suddenly decided to go back to Baza? He had left without making any plans or arrangements and she had no idea where he intended to stay or when he intended to return to Mojacar. Still he did have his mobile with him so he could contact her if, and when he needed to. Contacting him would be less easy, she reasoned, as he seldom remembered to switch the thing on.

Helen and Carol had never been close. Carol was not someone that Helen would have chosen as a friend. They were very different and it was only because she had married her brother that Helen spent any time in her company. According to Helen, Carol made too much of her "perfect" house and family. The girls had gone to private school in Edinburgh before inevitably gaining good exam grades and moving on to University. Yes, their house was large and in the right part of town, but there was no need to flaunt their good fortune in Helen's opinion. Helen was single by her own choice, thank you very much, she would say. Her flat was small but modern and always immaculately tidy. There had been several boyfriends. None of the relationships had lasted more than a couple of years and the breakups, when they occurred, had without exception been instigated by Helen. Carol had found it difficult to hide her feelings on that particular matter.

It was early afternoon as Helen made her way down from the villa towards the beach. The grillos were making their familiar high-pitched screech from the scrub lands between the properties. The un-made road was wide enough for single file slow moving vehicles but the surface was uneven and pot-holed. Her dark sun glasses obscured her vision and slowed her progress as she picked her way along the edge of the track, her sandals constantly scuffing through the dry grit and scorched grass throwing up puffs of dust. She knew the route well and she had taken the sensible precaution of donning a wide brimmed sun hat and a liberal application of high factor sun cream. The short, steep track passed by several communities, all very similar in layout to the one that Villa Campomar belonged to. Within five minutes or so Helen was at the main road which ran along the beach front. The road, as usual, was busy with cars and vans travelling in seemingly unending streams. Eventually a short gap appeared and Helen darted across.

The beach sloped gently down to the motionless Mediterranean with the white sand stretching as far as the eye could see in both directions, the view broken only by the occasional inviting beach bar. Warm sand entered her open-toe sandals and burned at the soles of her feet as she made her way towards the inviting shade of El Arbol

Verde. Helen knew the café-bar well. She had spent many summer evenings there with her brother and Carol in the past and had become friendly with one of the waiters, Manuel, who she kept in touch with by email and text. The name of the bar had always amused her. There was very little nearby that could conceivably provide any shade and there certainly were no trees. She had been told that the previous owners had run a bar in a village in Essex called the Green Tree and had carried forward the Spanish form of the name to their new property in Mojacar.

The menu del dia, together with a list of bocadillos and raciones were written in chalk on a board outside El Arbol Verde. Helen stepped inside removing her hat and sun glasses. The tall sun-tanned waiter, who was talking to a group of young women sitting at a table in the corner, turned around on hearing her enter. A wide smile immediately spread across his face.

"Helen! How good to see you again. I got your email and wondered when you would come down to see me. Is your brother not with you?"

"It's good to see you too Manuel. Sam has gone to Baza so I have been left on my own for a few days", she replied fixing her eyes directly on his face to gauge his reaction.

Manuel Fuentes was in his mid-forties. His active job had helped him retain a slim figure and his neatly cut jet-black hair (which Helen had always suspected as having been dyed) was pulled tightly off his face forming a short pony tail at the back. He was dressed immaculately. His white shirt, neatly pressed black trousers, well-polished shoes and the general care that he had taken to his appearance reflected the professional way that he approached his work. His efficiency was evident. Most of the tables were occupied but those that were not were clean and tidy, free from the usual discarded clutter found at most other similar beach bars.

Manuel walked towards Helen but his attention was drawn by a couple sitting at a table near the cigarette machine. The man signalled with a wave of his hand and silently mouthed the words "La cuenta".

"One moment Helen, I need to prepare the bill for this gentleman. I will be with you shortly."

Helen took a seat at one of the unoccupied tables that looked out through the large windows onto the beach where a few sun bathers lay stretched out and motionless on their loungers while others sat below sunshades either reading or gazing out to sea.

# 6

## JABALCON AND FURTHER REFLECTION

José and Carlos were losing patience. They had been waiting in the finca since first light.

"Where is he José? He should have been here hours ago."

"Patience Carlos, Hernandez is an important man; he will come when he can. Firstly, he no doubt has other business to attend to. Best keep your temper and show him some respect when he arrives. I have heard that he can be dangerous to deal with if angered."

"What is this Hernandez like José? Have you met him?"

"Few people have. I have never seen nor spoken directly to him. He sends no emails or letters that can be traced, communicating only by public telephone phone through an associate."

"So why is he meeting us in person today?"

"I have no idea Carlos, but I assume that he wishes to speak to us on an issue of some importance regarding the arrival of the contact from Manchester who is now in Baza and that what he has to say is intended for our ears only."

From the window of the finca the two men could see the narrow road that led down the mountain through the olive groves to the village of Zucar. Beyond Zucar lay the Murcia Granada autopista and the whirling blades on top of the tall white columns at the wind farm. On the other side of the motorway they could just make out houses on the outskirts of Baza, partially hidden by the heat haze. "Come away from the window, we may as well make ourselves comfortable. Food has been left for us in the fridge and there is a bottle of wine on the table in the kitchen", José added.

———

Sam had settled into a comfortable hotel in Baza. He couldn't quite bring himself to use the one that he had previously booked in to with Carol. Instead he had opted for Hostal Las Galletas, a small, friendly, family run hotel in the new block of buildings in Calle Antonio Machado just off Calle Alamillos. Sam and Carol had adopted the name "Bank Street" for Calle Alamillos, partially because of the difficulty they had in pronouncing the Spanish name but mainly because of the abundance of banks on both sides of the street.

The room was on the first floor and was neat and modern. Two single beds, a TV set, a chair and a desk made up the only furniture but there was a built-in wardrobe and en-suite facilities. The walls were freshly decorated and the air conditioning functioned efficiently. There wasn't much of a view from the window. It looked down into the narrow street and opposite was the back of the cinema. Sam smiled as he remembered going there with Carol. The picture being shown was "Jonny English" portrayed by Rowan Atkinson. It was dubbed in Spanish, of course, but it hadn't mattered to them that they could barely follow the dialogue as the basis for the humour was all in the action.

Sam had placed his small Dama de Baza statuette on the table. It seemed appropriate to have brought it with him. As he gazed out of the window his thoughts again turned to that fateful day in Florence. He had returned to the café in Plaza della Signria at about 6.15pm where he and Carol had arranged to meet. There was no point in going in since Carol was due to arrive at 6.30pm and they would be making their way immediately to the restaurant on the other side of the river. Besides it was a warm evening and from the café doorway Sam had a good view across the Plaza to watch for her arriving. The Plaza was busy with people weaving about. Many seemed to be simply strolling aimlessly while others quickly dodged between them with more obvious purpose in mind. By twenty-to-seven Sam had become a bit more concerned. Carol was always punctual and unless she turned up very soon, they would be pressed to be on time for their restaurant booking. It was about then that Sam had thought that he had better check inside the café. Perhaps she had arrived early and was waiting inside for him. Looking around inside there was no sign of his wife. Various thoughts flowed through his head; had he been mistaken about the arrangement? Had they said that they would meet at the Restaurant? or perhaps outside the Uffizi? No, it was definitely here at the café and there was no doubt about the time. They had arranged 6.30pm.

Sam became more anxious as the time moved on to 6.50pm. He had no doubt in his mind regarding the time as he had been glancing at his watch every few minutes. There was still no sign of her. Sam decided that he should phone. Taking his mobile out of his jacket pocket he reflected, "This was so unlike Carol. Something must have occurred to delay her." He dialled her from his contacts list so there was no possibility of getting the number wrong. Her phone rang out without being answered and went to message mode. "Carol, Sam here. Where are you? I am waiting for you at the café as we arranged."

Sam had gone back into the café and left a quickly written message with the girl at the counter. The message simply stated that he was going on to the restaurant via the Uffizi: hoping that he would find her on the way: but if they were to miss each other they would meet up at the restaurant.

It was only a few minutes' walk from the café to the Uffizi. Gone were the former queues. The large wooden entrance doors were firmly locked shut. The museum was already closed. Sam checked the notice at the entrance,

"8.15am – 6.50pm, Tuesday – Saturday, last entry 45 minutes before closing." He had dialled her mobile again. Still there was no reply.

The most obvious answer, Sam had concluded, was that Carol had for some reason left the museum early and had had to go back to the hotel and was waiting there for him. Why she was not answering his calls was still strange. He turned around quickly and set off towards their hotel on Via Della Scala.

———

As the two men sipped their second large glass of wine in the kitchen at the back of the finca on Jabalcon, they heard the loud crunching of the gravel outside the front door as the Mercedes 4x4 braked and pulled up. Almost immediately there was a loud confident rap of the metal knocker on the wooden door, clearly demanding urgent attention. Both men looked up with a start.

"Hernandez!" exclaimed José with some trepidation. "Answer it quickly and let him in Carlos."

Carlos unbolted the door and cautiously swung it open. Standing in the door-way was a tall, slim, fair skinned woman in her early fifties. Although not conventionally beautiful, her face projected an inner confidence and intelligence that many would find attractive. Her expression was intense and with her dark piercing eyes she was already quickly weighing up Carlos. She wore a smart black trouser suit and an expensive gold watch reflected in the sunlight. Slung over her shoulder was a large leather carrier bag and down by her side she held a bright red, wide brimmed sun hat. She handed the bag and hat to Carlos stepping past him into the room.

"You expected Hernandez," she said as a faint smile passed over her lips, amused to have taken the men by surprise. "He has important business to attend to in Granada. He has sent me with your instructions."

# 7

## PHONE CALL

Helen woke early the next morning in Villa Campomar. She turned to face Manuel but he was still asleep. The bedroom was littered with their discarded clothes and on the table in the corner were the remains of several bottles of Rioja and two glasses stained with the red wine from the night before. The curtains were drawn making the room dark and difficult for her to gauge the time of day. Helen's head throbbed as she pulled back the bed sheets and stepped onto the tile floor. Manuel gave a grunt and turned over as he went back to sleep. Helen pulled on the jumper, jeans and a pair of soft shoes that were lying on the floor and made her way through to the living room. She opened the curtains and immediately the bright sun flooded into the room. Shading her eyes from the glare she turned to look at the clock on the opposite wall. It was 10.30am.

"Oh my God. It is a good job that Sam isn't around to see this mess." Helen went back into the bedroom and started to clear the bottles and glasses and generally to tidy the room up a bit. "Manuel, you lazy lump! wake up and help me put this place back in some order."

Manuel sat bolt upright. "Sam hasn't come back has he?" he said looking anxiously through into the living room.

"No, but he could at any time. Have you seen my phone? He may have left a message." Frantically turning over a pile of newspapers on the floor, Helen came across her phone. "No messages, but that still doesn't mean that he is not on his way here now. I need to go down to the supermarket and buy in some things before he comes back. It would be best if he weren't to find you here like this if he arrives this morning. Let yourself out and I will come down to the Arbol Verde later this afternoon. Hasta luego." With that she opened the front door, turning to give a smile to Manuel and then swiftly made her way to the supermarket.

As she made her way down the lane, she thought to herself, "Sam likes Manuel and I know he is happy that we are friends. I just don't particularly want my brother knowing how good friends we are."

It was nearly 12.00 when she returned to the Villa laden down with two full bags of groceries and replacement wine. She was relieved to see that Manuel had gone. She had not relished the thought of having to explain his presence and overnight stay to her brother.

"It's not that Sam would strongly disapprove. I know that it is ridiculous but I just don't feel comfortable sharing too many details of my life with him. I may be in my 40's but he still treats me as his little sister," she thought.

In fact, Sam was not on his way back to Mojacar, he was still in Baza. He needed time on his own to think through the events in Florence three years before.

He remembered returning to the hotel on Via Della Scala, checking their room and speaking to the young man at the reception desk but no sign nor word of Carol. It was by then nearly 7.30pm when he again set out towards the restaurant where he had booked the table for them earlier that day. Surely, she would be waiting for him there, her mobile phone out of charge. Sam was aware that he had walked briskly towards the restaurant but he found it difficult to remember any detail. By this time, he had become very anxious and his focus was simply on getting to the restaurant as quickly as possible. It crossed his mind that perhaps there had been some accident or perhaps Carol had taken ill and was now in hospital. At the restaurant his worst fears had been realised. She was not there either and the waiter that he spoke to confirmed that she had not been in the restaurant. It was by then plain to Sam that there was some serious problem and his mind had raced through what he should do next. He had little Italian to cope with the emergency that was unfolding.

The waiter had been aware that Sam was worried and offered to help. "I will speak to the manager and ask him to make a call to the police station for you. If there has been any accident and if your wife has been taken to hospital then they will be able to check on your behalf. Take a seat. This may take some time. You say that she was visiting the Uffizi this afternoon?"

The rest was a bit hazy in Sam's mind. He felt that the events of the following few days were just a bad dream. The police had, of course, found nothing to report and Sam had been asked to call in at the station the next morning for an update. Helpfully the waiter from the restaurant had gone with him to assist with the language. The police officer had taken them into a side office, told Sam that their investigations had failed to shed any light on his wife's whereabouts and then he had asked a number of questions:

"Did your wife know anyone in Florence?"

"Was there any reason that she may have decided to go off on her own?"

"Did she have her passport with her?"

"What was she wearing when you last saw her?"

Sam had answered "no" to each of the first three questions and then, with some degree of effort, gave as good a description of the clothes that Carol had on, as he could remember. The police officer informed Sam that there was little that they could do for the moment and asked if he had a recent photo of his wife that they could have. Sam had handed over the memory card from his camera. Carol was on many of the photographs that he had taken since arriving in Florence.

"When do you intend to return to Britain?"

"Our flight is booked for tomorrow afternoon from Piza to Manchester but I will cancel it."

"Please do not leave Florence until we tell you. I will have the flight checked to see if your wife turns up and boards. Meanwhile I have registered your wife as a missing person."

She didn't board the plane the next day and Sam had been called back to the police station for further questions.

"Did your wife take her mobile phone with her?"

"What is her number?"

"Did she seem distressed or anxious in any way when you left her?"

Sam had answered all of these

"Could you give me an account of what you did and where you were between the time that you last saw your wife up to the call that we received from the restaurant?"

"Why do you need to know that?"

"Purely routine sir but we now know from the security cameras at the Uffizi that your wife did not enter there at the time you said she did."

————

Helen was sitting on the terrace at Villa Campomar reading a book that she had bought earlier while at the supermarket. She was only paying partial attention to the story line and she was thinking that perhaps it was time that she made her way down to the Arbol Verde to see Manuel when her mobile phone rang indicating that it had received a message. "Sam at last," she thought as she laid the book face down to keep her place. She walked over to the table and picked up the phone. The "message received" WhatsApp was flashing and she pressed the read option. She read the short message which caused her to take a sharp intake of breath and immediately drop the phone onto the tiled floor.

It read:

*Helen, please get this message to Sam. I know he is somewhere in Baza. Tell him to meet me below the church in the village of Freila at 3pm on Friday. It is important. Tell him to bring the statuette of the Dama de Baza with him and to come alone.*

*Carol.*

# 8

## FREILA

Crowds flocked around the procession in the street below Sam's hotel window. The scene was both ordered and chaotic. The focal point was the large statue of the virgin carried on a trestle by twelve young men. The men moved slowly; their backs bent by the heavy load that they were supporting. Every few yards, at the signal blown on a whistle from the procession leader, they stopped and laid the trestle on the ground. After only a few seconds respite the whistle would sound again and the men would take hold of the support poles, raise the statue off the ground and slowly move on. The rest of the procession followed behind spilling into, and mixing with the crowds that filled the pavements on either side of the narrow street.

Sam had just heard his sister's news. He had switched on his mobile and called her with the intention of letting her know that he intended to return to Mojacar later in the day. Now he was stunned. He gazed at the scene unfolding outside his window but his thoughts were elsewhere. *"Could the message that Helen had received really have come from Carol?* The main part of the procession had moved on, turning the sharp corner at the bottom of the street and was now out of sight but the chaos of the milling crowds that followed on behind was still there.

It was Wednesday. The message indicated that the meeting was to take place on Friday in Freila. Sam needed time to think. He needed to make some sense of the unexpected turn of events. Certainly he would go to the church, but he would not allow himself to expect too much. It could all be some cruel hoax.

Sam reasoned that an early visit to Freila to check out the location of the proposed meeting was required. There were no other priorities and he decided to go immediately. The road out of Baza leading north was signposted Pozo Alcon and Cuaves del Campo. Sam followed this road as it passed through the village of Zucar with the steep sided mountain Jabalcon dominating views to the right. At the roundabout he took a left turn. A sign at the side of the road indicated that Freila was 3km further on. The road twisted and turned with glimpses of Embalse de Negratin, a long narrow reservoir, passing into and out of view. Sam was only partially aware of his surroundings. He was turning the news from his sister over and over in his mind.

Eventually the road descended a steep hill and at the bottom Sam could see ahead of him, a junction leading off to the left. The sign at the junction indicated that the road led to Freila. Sam slowed the car down, engaged second gear and turned up the hill into the village. The main street of the village was narrow but there was little traffic about to cause any difficulty. In fact, there was very little sign of life. Sam glanced at his watch. "Of course, it's just gone 2pm, the hottest part of the day. Everyone is inside", he realised. In the centre of the village the sign for the church pointed down a steep hill. Cautiously Sam manoeuvred the hired car down the narrow lane, the sun reflecting off of the bright red bodywork into his eyes making the going extra difficult. The lane ended in a T-junction and Sam made the sharp left turn. He was driving slowly and in first gear. Almost immediately he had to turn sharply again, this time to the right. The small white church with its bell tower was straight ahead. Sam parked outside in the yard and got out of the car to look around. The main entrance to the church was locked but Sam could see immediately that the building was lovingly cared for. The freshly painted walls shone in the sunlight and high above, in the tower, the large metal bell looked as if it had been recently polished. Sam walked around one side of the building. The church was perched on the edge of a cliff and was surrounded by a low wall with metal railings. Sam looked over the wall; the view was magnificent. About 100ft below the valley was filled with olive trees and beyond, and on the other side, a track led upwards, twisting and turning past small fincas. The still, blue water of the reservoir could be clearly made out in the distance.

Sam paused to take in the beauty of his surroundings. Looking down he could see the maze of smart buildings that made up the village. On closer inspection he could see that many of them were cave houses. Only the entrances and the small front gardens of these were visible but they were clearly well cared for, smart and tidy. Sam pondered how old these dwellings could be and what the insides must be like. He wondered why this particular spot should have been chosen for the meeting.

At the far end of the wall a flight of steep steps spiralled downwards. These led to a second balcony below the level of the church, cut into the face of the rock. From here a further set of steps led down to the valley below.

"It's quite a view." Sam was startled by the deep voice from behind him. Turning around he was faced by a tall, well-dressed man. "You are English and want to buy a cave house?"

"No on both counts. I'm from Edinburgh and I am only passing through"

Recovering his composure Sam looked more closely at the stranger. His hair was grey but he didn't look more than about 50. There was a broad smile on his face and his skin gave the appearance of someone who had spent much of his time in the sun. His accent was indistinct. Sam thought him to be either British or Australian. His appearance was neat but closer inspection his clothes looked a bit worn. "My name's Joe, Joe Walker. I run a small estate agency in Baza but I am originally from Essex. I moved here about

10 years ago, before house prices in Spain took a tumble. "I assumed that you were looking around at property on the market. I am sorry if I startled you."

"You did a bit," Sam confessed. "I already have a holiday home in Mojacar."

"Mojacar is full of Brits-expats and holiday makers. You want to move here, to real Spain," Joe laughed as he gave his advice.

"Actually, you might be able to help me," Sam ventured. "I need to stay in Freila for a few days. There are clearly no hotels. I did pass a hostal on the way in near Zucar, but I need to be in the village. Do you know of anyone who would let me rent, for say 1 week?"

"There is a two-bedroom cave for sale a five-minute walk from here. It's in a great spot with views over the valley into the campo, very quiet. The owners wouldn't mind you renting it short term. The market is slow at the moment. I have the keys in my van if you would like to take a look at it. I'm parked outside the church."

Sam followed Joe back to his van. It was parked beside Sam's hired car.

"It's pointless having too good a vehicle in the village. The tracks are narrow and badly surfaced. As you can see from the van, you are liable to end up with a few dents and scratches." Joe remarked.

It wasn't long before Sam could see what he meant. The track twisted and turned by what appeared to be randomly positioned buildings and then quickly descended past the entrances to a series of cave houses. Just as quickly the track then turned back upwards. The change was so abrupt that the van body screeched as the vehicle chassis bottomed out. Joe was unperturbed and Sam reasoned that this must be a regular occurrence. Eventually Joe brought the van to a stop tight in against a low wall. "We need to get out and walk the last bit," he advised. "This area of the village is called Barrio Pozo, which means the well district, but I have never been able to find any wells here."

Sam got out of the van and looked over the low wall. The view of the valley was magnificent and he could see a steep narrow path with steps leading downwards. "The owners put the steps in and wanted to have them wider, but the path is a right of way down into the campo and the route had to be kept suitable for the donkeys," Joe explained. The two men slowly descended the path. Joe was in the lead with Sam closely behind. About half way down the path turned away from the cliff face and for the first time Sam could see the entrance to the cave house that he was being taken to. Outside there was a small but well attended patio area. The rock was freshly painted white. To the left of the door was a small, barred window and further round to the right he could see that there was a balcony area attached to the cave house which was protected by a covered roof jutting out from the rock face. "It can get quite cold here in the winter and snow is not uncommon in December and January. The rest of the year the temperature hovers around 35 and can climb into the 40s. However, the temperature inside the cave remains about 18 to 20 throughout the year. It is one of the advantages of this type of property," Joe pointed out.

Joe inserted the key into the metal door and swung it open. Holding the vertical strands of the fly screen aside he invited Sam to step inside. "I think you will be pleasantly surprised."

On entering the cave house out of the sun Sam was immediately aware of the temperature difference. The heavy door led directly into the living room. It was cool and inviting. The internal walls were painted white and small alcoves had been cut in the walls and various small ornaments had been carefully placed in these. Paintings of workers in the fields hung on the walls. The furniture was simple but adequate. A glass table with metal chairs was positioned against one of the walls and two comfortable looking armchairs sat on either side of a log burning stove. The floor was tiled and had a colourful wool rug as a centre piece.

"The rugs in the cave came from the Alpajarra region on the other side of Granada. Off to your right is the kitchen which is fitted out with a fridge and cooker. The door to your left leads into a double bedroom with a bathroom beyond. There is also a door in there which opens out onto a balcony. The door straight ahead takes you into another double bedroom which has its own separate toilet and shower room." Joe had fallen naturally into his estate agent mode. "If you want to rent it for a week, I can get the owners to give you a preferential rate as a possible buyer, say 150 euros."

"I haven't said that I am thinking of buying, but yes I think that it is perfect for my stay here in the village."

# 9

---

## FRIDAY

---

The next two days passed peacefully but slowly. The village was quiet and the cave comfortable, both of which suited Sam. From the small patio area outside the cave Sam had a clear view of the surrounding fields with their olive bushes and beyond to the gentle up slope on the other side of the valley. The outlook was stunning but Sam was lost in his own thoughts. Friday could not come quickly enough. His phone rang and he quickly answered it.

"Sam, it's Helen. I'm coming up to Freila to be with you."

"No, don't do that, I'm fine. The meeting is tomorrow at 3 and I have to go alone. It is more than likely a cruel hoax of some kind in any case.

"That's what worries me. Either way, if it's genuine or a hoax I think that you will need support."

"You don't have any way to get here. I have the car."

"I'll ask Manuel if I can borrow his and will be with you by 1." She hung up before Sam could reply.

––––––––––

Sam woke early on Friday. He had slept little and decided that he was as well just to get up. He showered and dressed quickly and took his phone outside. The walls of the cave were too thick to allow messages to penetrate. Immediately the phone indicated that were two messages waiting. He opened the first. The number was not one that he was familiar with. It read "Change of plan, meeting brought forward to 12.00" The second was from Helen, "Sam, I am not going to be able to meet you until nearer 2. Manuel's car is in the garage for repair, so I need to organise a hire car, Sorry. We should still have an hour together before the meeting. I am determined to be with you."

Sam answered Helen's message immediately. "Just make your way up when you can. Set your satnav for Calle San Isidro and follow the track to the end. The cave house that I have rented is just below. If I am not in you will find the key below the mat at the door. My meeting has been brought forward."

Sam spent the rest of the morning sitting outside the cave looking across the valley and contemplating what might be ahead of him. He had mixed feelings of trepidation and excitement but desperately tried to temper his hopes and expectations. At 11.40 he could sit still no longer and decided to make his way round to the church. It only took 5 minutes. He passed no-one on the way. Two vehicles occupied the paved area outside the church, a light blue Mercedes 4x4 and a white van. Both were unoccupied and the area surrounding the church was deserted apart from a stray cat that ran across the paving slabs and then disappeared up one of the cobbled streets leading to the village square. Sam walked to the railings on the far side of the church yard and looked over into the valley below. A gentle breeze was blowing but there was no sign of life. A steep staircase led downwards from one corner. Sam checked his watch; it was 11.50am and felt inside his pocket, checking that he had the Dama de Baza statuette with him. Slowly he made his way down the stairs, holding on to the railings on either side. His heart was racing.

# 1 0

Signing the paperwork and taking out the necessary insurances for the hire car had taken Helen longer than she had anticipated, but at last she was ready to be on her way. She phoned Sam to give him an update, but there was no reply. "*Typical of my brother*," she thought, "*Probably has it turned off.*" Helen set the satnav to the details that Sam had given her and set off.

Helen stopped in a layby just after leaving the motorway exit for the village and tried Sam's number again. Still no response so she continued on down the narrow one-way lanes leading towards Calle San Isidro stopping briefly at the church square. It was deserted and she drove on.

*"I'm glad that Sam made his way down here before me. It doesn't look suitable for cars,"* she thought. As she turned the sharp corner into Calle San Isidro, Sam's car came into view, parked tight against the low white wall. She parked behind it and made her way cautiously down the narrow path towards the cave house. Immediately she could see why her brother had chosen to rent it, the view of the valley from the small patio was breath-taking. There was no sign of her brother, but the key was below the mat as he had said it would be. Helen tried Sam's number again. Still no reply. This time she left a message, "Where are you Sam?" and then opened the door, pushed aside the mosquito screen and went inside.

Helen looked around. Sam was not the tidiest of individuals, dishes lay in the sink and the tiled floor looked like it could do with a good clean with a mop. *"I can't just wait about here."* she thought. She went back outside, locked the door and put the key back where she had found it. Helen climbed the steep path back to where her car was parked and then made her way towards the church square. A dog barked from inside one of the cave houses as she passed by. The church square was still deserted, as it had been when she had first driven past. She walked to the railings at the far end and looked down. The open stairway leading to the platform below was clearly visible, but it was impossible to see much of the platform itself. Helen walked over to the stairs, peered down and took hold of the railing at the side. It was hot from the sun and she withdrew her hand instantly. Cautiously she made her way down the stairs, glancing nervously back up after the first few steps. The stairs led onto the platform. The doors and windows of three, as yet unfinished properties, lay in the shade slightly below the overhang from the square above. It looked as if they were destined to be shop outlets, their windows were covered in whitewash and it was impossible to see inside. Helen tried each of the doors in turn. They were locked. She climbed back up the stairs to the church square avoiding contact with the hot handrail. Near the top she thought that she could hear voices just above her so she quickened her step. Two women were sitting on one of the benches deep in conversation, their shopping bags were on the ground at their side. Helen went up to them and then, after briefly passing the normal pleasantries, she gave them a description of her brother and enquired if they had seen him. They looked at each other and the older of the two asked, "Has he has moved into the house below Calle San Isidro?"

News obviously travelled fast in the small close-knit community. "Yes," Helen was pleased to be making some headway. "Have you seen him today?" The women looked at each other and shrugged their shoulders. "No, sorry." Helen thanked them and since there was no one else about to ask, she walked back towards the cave house.

As she passed the cave with the dog it barked loudly again. "Oh, be quiet!" she asserted with a rather uncharacteristic show of exasperation. Helen used the key to open the cave house door again and went in. She decided that she would look around more thoroughly this time in case Sam had left a note for her somewhere. She checked in the larger of the two bedrooms. There was nothing out of place. She assumed that Sam was not making use of this one. The second bedroom was different. The bed was unmade and clothes were carelessly strewn about the floor. The book that her brother was in the middle of reading lay in the alcove behind the bed together with a pair of reading glasses and an alarm clock. "*This is more like Sam,*" she thought as she picked up the discarded clothes and placed them on the chair in a corner of the room. But there was no note. Helen had a closer look at the alarm clock. It was set for 6am. "*Unlike Sam to get up so early but then I am sure that he was anxious about today's meeting.*" Next she checked the small bathroom leading off from the bedroom. Again it was untidy, but there was nothing to give her a clue as to where Sam might be. She moved back into the living room. Newspapers were scatted about the room. She arranged these into a tidy pile and placed them on the small table beside the fireplace. "*Never thought of cave houses having fireplaces and chimneys.*" Helen went through to the kitchen and began washing up the cups in the sink, just for something to keep her occupied. She could see the view of the valley from the kitchen window. A stray cat passed by. "*Nothing I can do until I hear from Sam,*" she thought. "*He has probably gone up to the village square to get some food in for us,*" she reassured herself, but she couldn't conceal her concern.

----

Chief Inspector Antonio Ferrer Garcia looked down at the body that lay slumped in the corner of Calle de las

Piedras Pequeñas, a narrow alleyway in Granada that led up from Carrera del Darro into the area known as the Albacin. The Chief Inspector had been a member of the National Police based in the city for 12 years. In that time, he had been called out to deal with numerous break-ins, robberies and other such incidents but this was only his second contact with a brutal murder and it made him feel sick to the stomach. The victim, a middle-aged man, had been shot from close range through the back of his head. The circumstances were similar in Antonio's previous case two months earlier; the victim shot in the back of the head with no attempt made to hide the body; the perpetrator as yet unknown.

It was now 3 in the afternoon and, according to the initial report that Antonio had been handed, this latest victim had been dead for only a few hours. The alley was in the shade, the high stone walls on either side providing protection from the glare of the sun. The outline of the Alhambra was just visible on the other side of the river Darro. Inspector Garcia was accompanied by two colleagues, Fermin Casillas and Jaime Hidalgo, both younger than him by a good few years and both considerably less experienced. Antonio turned his back on the scene.

"The body has been brought and dumped here, probably not long ago", suggested Fermin. "This is a fairly well used alleyway. It looks like it was intended that the body be found easily. There has been no attempt to cover it up. A local resident, Pascual Peredes made the discovery while out walking his dog around 2.30pm. He is waiting in the police car down in Carrera del Darro to speak to you."

"You seem very distant Inspector", observed Jaime.

Antonio continued to stare down the alleyway and across to the Alhambra. "I know who this is, and probably why he was murdered."

———

The loud rap on the door made Helen jump. She had been dozing lightly on one of the chairs in the main room in the cave. She glanced at the clock on the wall. It was 4.30pm.

"Sam, at last", she thought then quickly realised that he would have his own key. She opened the door and the large frame of the uniformed police officer startled her. Immediately behind him was a female officer.

"Helen Crawford?", he enquired. "We need you to come with us to the police station in Baza".

# 11

## BAZA POLICE STATION

The fast drive to the police station in Baza only took 10 minutes. Traffic moved aside to allow the police car with its flashing light and siren through. During the journey Helen had tried to question the two officers, but they were unwilling, or unable, to provide her with any answers.

Baza police station is a modern, concrete, two storey building located in a short cul-de-sac just off Calle Alamillos in the centre of the town. The outside of the building proudly displays two large Spanish flags and fixed above the entrance in bold letters is the sign "Comisaría". The two officers quickly ushered Helen inside and past the reception desk. "You are to meet Inspector Manriquez in the office which is first on the right at the top of the stairs."

Helen quickly climbed the stairs, knocked loudly on the door and immediately entered the office.

The small, dimly lit, square room was sparsely furnished. The walls were decorated in a faded white emulsion. There was a window on the far wall which was partially obscured by a half open, twisted, venetian blind. A solitary wooden table sat in the middle of the room. The table, like the rest of the room had seen considerable service, probably as an interrogation area. There were two plastic chairs, one on either side of the table and sat in one of these was Sam.

"Sam, thank god, you have had me so worried. What the hell is going on?" Before Sam could answer her another person entered the room behind Helen.

"Ah, Helen Crawford, I am very pleased to meet you. Your brother told us you were likely to be at the cave house in Freila. I am Inspector Manriquez, Leandro Manriquez. I am so sorry that I must rush off. I have to meet with a senior officer in Granada. Sam will explain. I have asked that you be brought tea. I know how you British enjoy your tea", and with that he quickly turned and left. Sam looked across at his sister, the concern obvious in her eyes. "Sit down Helen and I will try to bring you up to date." Helen did as he suggested.

"The first thing to say is that the message apparently sent by Carol turned out to be no more than a cruel hoax. It was designed to ensure that I would turn up at the arranged meeting, which I of course did."

"Who sent the message and why was the time changed?"

"The first was the message from a Granada based gang called Salón Oscuro, I found this out this afternoon from Inspector Manriquez. The second, bringing the time of the meeting forward by two hours, was from the police in Granada. They wanted to ensure that I was safely out of the way by 2pm while they waited to see who would turn up."

"This isn't making much sense. Why did Salón Oscuro want to meet you? How did they know that you were here in Spain and where do the police fit in to all of this?"

"The police have been closely following Salón Oscuro. The Granada police have a mole working within the gang and he has been passing important information on to them. There has apparently been a power struggle within Salón Oscuro culminating in the shooting of the former leader. The new leader is a man who operates under the assumed name of Hernandez. Very few of the gang are reported to have actually met him. He is said to be ruthless and probably responsible for the murder of the former leader."

"That doesn't explain how Salón Oscuro knew about your movements, or why they wanted to contact you", Helen prompted.

"My upcoming lecture at Granada University has been well publicised and the travel arrangements were made by the university, remember? Any number of people had access to this information. Why they wanted to contact me will become clear shortly if you let me continue."

At that moment the door of the office opened and a young girl came in with a tray of biscuits and two mugs of tea.

"Why do the Spanish assume that we all drink tea Sam? I for one would rather have a stiff whisky at this moment in time."

"Yes of course Helen, I promise I will take you for one. The rest of what I have to tell you is based upon what Inspector Manriquez has felt able to divulge to me so the details are a bit sketchy. The police here in Baza were alerted to the meeting arrangements via a phone call from a Chief Inspector in Granada, whose name I can't recall for the moment. It was the Baza police that picked me up at 12 and brought me here. After that, apparently, officers from both the Baza and Granada forces lay in wait outside the church in Baza and apprehended two minor gang members acting suspiciously outside the church. Both men were known to the police who had been looking for them in connection with several breaking and entering cases. The men were interviewed separately and both of them decided independently to co-operate. Probably expecting some sort of a sentencing deal if they did. They gave the police officers the location of a finca on a mountain road near Zucar, which was where I was to be taken."

Helen found staying quiet during Sam's version of events difficult, so she intervened. "But why you Sam? What did they want you for?"

"Patience sis, I'm getting to that. You remember the title on the flier circulated by the University advertising the talk that I shall be giving in just over two weeks', "Pattern Recognition as an Aid to Code Breaking." Well it seems that Hernandez had managed to acquire what would appear to be a coded message. It had been taken from the previous gang leader by Hernandez and he is very keen, to say the least, to have the code broken. It was the gang's intention to hold me at the finca until I had deciphered it. The police went in numbers to the finca but found it to be deserted. They turned the place over and apart from some sandwiches and water in the fridge all that they found was a leather carrier bag. Inside this was an A4 envelope containing a collection of photographs, all virtually the same, of a watch, a candle, a fan and a miniature statuette of the Dama de Baza, similar to the one that Carol and I bought and I have with me."

"Well that's that then Sam. I'm so sorry that the message from Carol was not genuine. You have had quite a time but you can now put all this behind you." There was real concern for her brother in her voice as she tried to take it in.

"Not quite sis. You see the police are equally keen to have the code broken. It could help in their investigations into the gang." Sam hesitated at this point but Helen knew exactly what was coming.

"They have asked you to help and you have agreed, haven't you?"

"I have two spare weeks before the lecture and flight home and I have said that I would try during that time. No promises that I will be successful but I will give it a go. I intend to stay at the cave in Freila to work on this. It is much more peaceful there than at the place in Mojacar and perfect for giving my undivided attention to the project."

"Why am I not surprised?" added Helen with a gentle hint of sarcasm.

A smile formed on Sam's face. "I knew that you would understand and you can go back to Mojacar. I don't want to get in the way of your budding romance."

"Your Spanish must be better than I thought it was. Isn't the language going to be a bit of a barrier to your code breaking effort?" Helen suggested.

"According to the police any coding is likely to be in English for a reason that they were unwilling to divulge. I think that this is another reason why they want me to assist them."

"Ok Sam, but just one last question. You are not in any danger here are you? Why did the Inspector have to dash off to Granada in such haste?"

"That's two questions sis. The answer to the first is why would I be? As far as the second is concerned, I have absolutely no idea. Now let's go for that drink."

# 1 2

## EL SALÓN OSCURO

Leandro Manriques parked his unmarked police car outside the main police station in Granada and immediately made his way to the office of Chief Inspector Antonio Garcia. The two men knew each other well and there was no need for preliminaries. Antonio indicated that Leandro should take a seat which he did.

"Thank you for your assistance this afternoon Leandro. That was a well-co-ordinated operation leading to a very fruitful outcome." The Chief Inspector paused briefly then continued, "I need to advise you of further developments."

"A body was discovered today in, Calle de las Piedras Pequeñas, an alleyway off Carrera del Darro. The victim had been shot at close range in the back of the head. There are obvious similarities linking this latest killing with the one earlier this month." He looked across at his colleague and then continued. "As you know Danny Thomson, the former leader of El Salón Oscuro, met his end in an identical manner, probably as the consequence of a power struggle. As part of our investigations we have learned quite a lot about Danny Thomson. He was born in the East End of London, June 20th 1968. He had a number of run-ins with the London police then moved to the Costa del Sol in 2005, lying low for three years. In 2008 Thomson joined a profitable extortion racket in Granada which was expanding rapidly. Recently we have been making progress on identifying the workings of the gang, mainly through information being passed to us from a mole who had successfully infiltrated the group."

The Chief Inspector paused, stood up and crossed to the office window. As he looked down into the street below with his back to Leandro he continued, "The body that we discovered today was that of the mole, Paco Bosque, one of our undercover officers and a personal friend of mine."

The two men remained silent for what seemed an age. Eventually Chief Inspector Garcia turned to his colleague, "The only solid lead that we have at the moment is the collection of photographs that we recovered from the deserted finca. This mathematician, Samuel Crawford, he has agreed to help us determine their significance, hasn't he?"

Without waiting for an answer, he went on, "They must be of some relevance. What chance do you think he has of deciphering them?"

"He has made us no promises, Antonio. I have given him copies of each photograph and he says that he will try. Personally, I can't see what can possibly be deduced from a random series of photographs of a fan, candle, statuette and watch. There doesn't appear to be any markings on the back of the photographs. If he is unsuccessful, then we may be no further forward, but we will have lost nothing." The Chief Inspector looked unconvinced. "If nothing else, it does free up my available resources to deal with the most important aspect, that of finding the individual, or individuals responsible for these two murders."

———————

Los Cantaros is a smart bar and restaurant in the centre of Baza. It was Friday evening and, as usual, Los Cantaros was busy with most of the tables in the bar area occupied. The long narrow room was alive with various conversations interspersed with loud laughing. At the back of the bar, other tables had been neatly set out for meals. Only a few of these were taken. It was still early for the Spanish to sit down to their evening meal. Sam and Helen had been lucky and had found a table in the bar area tucked away in a corner.

Helen looked across the table at her brother, the fifteen print copies spread out in front of them, "Well then, where do you propose to start?"

"Good question Helen. Any information to be gleaned from these must be contained in the differences between them. But first I need to determine the order that they should be in."

"You don't think that they are even in the correct order!" The enormity of the task ahead was becoming clear to Helen. "There must be hundreds of possibilities."

"Just over $1.18 \times 10^{11}$ actually. There are fifteen possibilities for which is the first, leaving fourteen possibilities for the second, thirteen for the third, twelve for the fourth and so on. If you multiply these all together, we get the number 12 followed by 11 zeros."

"What!"

"Obviously I need to cut this down if I am going to have any chance of even making a start."

"And how can you do that?"

"I need to look for groupings, subtle similarities in the pictures that suggest combinations and alignments. Look closely at the pictures. The candle is present in all of the pictures, sometimes it is lit and sometimes unlit. The fan is present in some pictures but not on others. The statuette is in all of the pictures, but in some it is on the right-hand side, and on others it is on the left. The watch is also in all of the pictures, but the time shown varies. You can help me summarise all these details in a table." Sam set an A4 sheet of paper down on the table and with a pencil divided it into two sets of five columns and eight rows, entering a heading and key above each of the columns. With Helen's help he summarised the details of each of the fifteen photographs in the rows of the table.

| Photo ref. no. | Fan<br>P present<br>A absent | Candle<br>L lit<br>U unlit | Time on watch | Statuette<br>LS left side<br>RS right side |
|---|---|---|---|---|
| 1 | A | L | 8.10 | RS |
| 2 | P | U | 5.40 | RS |
| 3 | A | L | 7.20 | RS |
| 4 | A | L | 6.30 | RS |
| 5 | P | U | 4.20 | RS |
| 6 | A | U | 3.15 | RS |
| 7 | P | L | 2.30 | RS |
| 8 | A | U | 5.25 | LS |
| 9 | P | U | 6.15 | RS |
| 10 | A | U | 2.15 | RS |
| 11 | P | L | 1.05 | RS |
| 12 | A | U | 4.30 | RS |
| 13 | A | U | 1.05 | RS |
| 14 | P | U | 3.45 | RS |
| 15 | P | U | 7.10 | RS |

"At least it is a start", he suggested folding the sheet up and putting it into his jacket pocket together with the photographs.

Helen thought for a moment then raised the question. "The statuette is of the Dama de Baza, similar to the one that you have Sam. Don't you think that is quite a coincidence?"

"I don't think that there is any significance in that. These little statuettes are on sale in this region in many of the shops. There must literally be thousands of them in circulation. Drink up and I will telephone for a taxi for us back to Freila. I presume that you won't drive back to Mojacar until tomorrow morning."

# 1 3

---

## WORK BEGINS

---

Sam woke the next morning unaware of the exact time. His bedroom in the cave was almost pitch black. Sam got out of bed and opened the shutter on the small widow. To his surprise light flooded into the room. "It must be later than I thought." He found his watch which confirmed his suspicion. It had gone 9.00am. He went through to the living room and discovered a note from his sister on the table. Helen's bedroom door was open and it was clear that she had already left.

Sam lifted the note. "Sam, it's 8.00am and I am ready to leave. I need to go back to Mojacar and I don't think that I can be of much help to you in deciphering the photographs. There is no sound coming from your room so it's fair to assume that you are still asleep and I don't want to wake you. You need to rest after the events of yesterday. I will call you once I get back to the coast.

Good luck with your project.

Helen."

Sam went back to his room and through to the small bathroom. The shower was warm and refreshing. Dressing quickly, he decided that a walk in the village, before it became too hot, would clear his head and set him up to start work on the photographs. He wanted to get to know the village better and the first priority would be to find somewhere to have breakfast. It's a steep climb from the cave up to the village main square so Sam took his time. It was an ideal opportunity to look around and take in the atmosphere of his surroundings. The narrow lanes turned and twisted their way around the randomly placed caves and buildings. Eventually the route levelled out and Sam crossed the main street and went into the pedestrianised main square. The elegantly named Plaza de San Marcos wasn't large but Sam was immediately impressed by the calm atmosphere that it generated. In the centre was a fountain surrounded by stone lions, a small replica of the one that he had seen in the Patio de Los Leones in the Alhambra in Granada. On the far side was the imposing two storey ayuntamiento, the town hall. In one corner of the square was a bar, and outside the bar, protected by large sun umbrellas, were a random selection of tables and chairs. Many of the tables were occupied by locals, drinking coffee from clear handle-less glasses, chatting and eating cheese and tomato tostadas. Sam smiled politely at a middle-aged couple sitting at one of the tables and was greeted with a formal, but friendly, "Buenos dias." He went into the bar, pushing the chain fly-screen to one side. The room that he entered was fairly large. It was square shaped, with a counter on the left and several tables set out to the right; these were empty, everyone obviously preferring to be outdoors in the sunshine. Despite no-one being in the room, a quiz show boomed out from the television in the far corner. The barman, who had been serving the tables outside, came back into the room carrying a tray full of plates and empty glasses which he put down on the counter.

"Señor Crawford, what I get you?"

"You know my name!"

"Is small pueblo, Freila, no. I hear many things in my bar."

"Your English is very good, better than my Spanish. Es mucho calor, hoy."

"I work five years in hotel at coast, Torremolinos, many British come there for holidays."

"You have learned well." Sam glanced at the menu board behind the bar, "I would like a cafe con leche and a bocadello de queso. I would like to have it at one of these inside tables out of the sun. I have some work to do."

"No problem señor."

"Oh, and would you mind turning the sound down on the TV?" Sam added.

The barman shrugged his shoulders, picked up the handset from the bar counter, pointed it at the screen and muted the sound. Sam sat down at a table in the corner, took the A4 sheet of paper with the photograph details from his pocket, unfolded it and laid it flat on the table in front of him.

The barman brought the coffee and cheese sandwich to the table. "This is your work Señor? You make timetable?"

"It's more of a puzzle that I have to try to solve."

"I make sure you able to concentrate on your puzzles Señor Crawford. No-one disturbs you in my bar."

After half an hour the barman returned to the table. "You want more coffee? Your puzzles not good señor? I take away all these crumpled papers for you?"

Sam had to admit to himself that he hadn't made much progress. The various scribbles on the discarded sheets of note paper bearing evidence to the fact. "I need to find some way to break the pictures down into groups," he thought. He pushed the A4 sheet to one side and looked at the barman. "Yes, another coffee might help me think, thanks."

The barman turned and went off to pour the coffee. Sam resumed his thoughts, "What are the details: The watch and the statuette are in all of the pictures while the fan and the candle are present in some but not all, so perhaps the fan and the candle are the key to arranging the groups." He tore a fresh page from his note book and wrote:

A possible grouping could be:

1. those with the fan and candle. There are 7
2. those with the candle but no fan. There are 8 of these.

Sam looked at what he had written. "That would certainly help if it were true, but I need some proof to be confident, and even then, I need some way of ordering the photographs within each group to make real progress."

The barman returned with the second coffee and quietly placed it on the table. "I don't disturb you with your puzzles." Sam was busily rewriting the picture details on a fresh sheet of A4 but this time arranged into the two groups that he had speculated.

| Group | Fan<br>p present<br>a absent | Candle<br>p present | Time on watch<br>hours, mins |
|---|---|---|---|
| 1 | p | p | 4.20 |
| 1 | p | p | 2.30 |
| 1 | p | p | 6.15 |
| 1 | p | p | 1.05 |
| 1 | p | p | 3.45 |
| 1 | p | p | 7.10 |
| 1 | p | p | 5.40 |
| 2 | a | p | 2.15 |
| 2 | a | p | 4.30 |
| 2 | a | p | 1.05 |
| 2 | a | p | 3.15 |
| 2 | a | p | 8.10 |
| 2 | a | p | 6,30 |
| 2 | a | p | 5.25 |
| 2 | a | p | 7.20 |

He was studying the new table when his phone rang. "Hello Sam, it's me. I said I would phone once I got back to Mojacar."

"Helen, thanks. How were the roads? Is everything ok in the house?"

"Yes, everything is fine. I would have phoned earlier but I had to go to the Supermercado for milk and bread,"

"Did you also pay a visit to the Arbol Verde beach bar?"

"Eh yes."

"Thought you might have, and how is Manuel?" Sam was only partly paying attention to the conversation. He was more intent on studying the A4 sheet in front of him.

"Manuel is not in the bar at the moment. The owner said that he was taking some time off to visit a sick aunt in Cordoba."

"That's good of him." Sam was still looking intently at the sheet. "Just a minute, that's interesting."

"Pardon Sam?"

"No, not Manuel or his sick aunt in Cordoba, I have noticed something with the photographs. I will call you back sometime tonight," and with that he hung up.

Sam looked again at his new notes. "This confirms the two groups, and not only that but the order of the photographs within each group." He sat back in his chair with a look of satisfaction on his face.

"You are well Señor Crawford, or have you drunk too much coffee?" the barman asked with some concern.

"I am fine, more than fine, you see the clue is in the hour hand on the watch."

The barman turned and went to tend to the customers outside, mumbling something under his breath about the sanity of the British.

What Sam had seen in the pictures that made up a group concerned the hour hand on the watch. Each hour, one, two three etc. was used once and only once. In the first group the hours depicted were one through to seven and in the second the hours ran from one to eight. He had his groups and the order of the pictures within each group. But now he had the harder task of deciphering the meaning.

# 14

## INITIAL INVESTIGATIONS

Chief Inspector Garcia made his way into the briefing room in the Granada police station. It was 8.30am and his team were already waiting for him. There were six officers assigned to the investigation including Fermin Casillas and Jaime Hidalgo, the two officers who had visited the crime scene with Antonio the day before. The Chief Inspector walked over to the desk at the far side of the room, laid down his notepad and the paper cup containing his half-drunk coffee and turned to face the assembled group.

"As you know we are treating the two murders, that of Danny Thomson, former gang leader of Salón Oscuro, and yesterday's killing of our colleague, Paco Bosque, who was working undercover within the gang, as related incidents, probably perpetrated by the same individual or individuals. The circumstances are similar. In both cases the victim was shot in the back of the head at close range and the body deliberately dumped where it would easily be found." The chief inspector paused and took a last sip of his coffee which had now turned cold. He looked around the room at the silent faces, tossed the empty paper cup into a bin, and continued. "The first victim, Danny Thomson was born in the East End of London on the 20th of June 1968. He was well known to the London police before he moved to the Costa del Sol in 2005. Sometime around 2008 Thomson came here to the city setting up the gang that we know as Salón Oscuro, specialising in protection rackets. Danny Thomson's body was discovered early in the morning of the 1st of August on a quiet street on the south side of the city by a resident returning from nightshift. We assume that the body was thrown from a car sometime during the night. There were no witnesses and forensics have been unable to provide us with any significant leads.

"The body of Paco Bosque, the second victim, was found yesterday at 2.30pm in an alleyway in the Albacin area of the city by Pascual Peredes, while out walking his dog. I have his statement." Antonio picked up his notepad and read, "My name is Pascual Peredes. I live at number 6, Plaza de las Flores, Granada. I left my house to take my dog for a walk at 2.15pm on Friday afternoon. I made my way down Calle de las Piedras to Carrera del Darro. It is a routine that I have followed since I got the dog two years ago. The Calle de las Piedras is narrow and there are high walls on either side. There is a flight of steps at the bottom end of the alleyway. It took me about 5 minutes to reach Carrera del Darro and the only person that I passed was a well-dressed woman walking the other way up the alleyway. She was wearing a black trouser suit. I did not see her face properly which was obscured by her large bright red sun hat. She was on her own. At the bottom of the alleyway I paused briefly for a smoke and then I remembered that I had intended to take a letter with me for posting. I would have noticed had anyone gone up Calle de las Piedras, but no-one did. I turned and made my way back up the alleyway. I walked slowly as it is steep. About half-way up, the alleyway takes a sharp turn to the right. The dog was pulling ahead heavily on the lead and barking loudly. On turning the corner, I discovered what was upsetting the dog. The still body of a man was slumped against the right-hand wall. At first, I thought he was either drunk, or asleep but when I moved closer it was clear that he was dead. It could have been no more than 20 minutes since I had passed the same spot on the way down."

Chief Inspector Antonio Garcia looked up from his notes, "The witness goes on to explain that he immediately went back to his house and phoned here, to the police station."

"Chief Inspector…," one of the team seemed anxious to raise a point.

"I will answer detail questions shortly, but let me continue because what I still have to say has a major bearing on this case. On Friday afternoon, ably assisted by Inspector Leandro Manriques and his officers in Baza, we successfully apprehended two minor members of the Salón Oscuro gang. They led us to a finca that the gang were using on the mountain track leading up Jabalcon and there we recovered a number of photographs which appear to be of some interest to the gang leadership. At the moment we don't know why this might be, but we suspect that they form some kind of coded message."

Antonio paused, partly to allow the information to be absorbed and partly for dramatic effect before he went on. "The two gang members informed us that they were visited at the finca by a woman who they said had close connections to the present leader of Salón Oscuro. The description that they gave of her suggests that she could be the woman who passed Pascual Peredes on Calle de las Piedras."

There was silence for a few seconds before Antonio continued. "Now I will take your questions."

"Chief Inspector, am I right in saying that the Plaza del Flores, where our witness lives, is at the top of the alleyway where the body was found, and that the only way into or out of the alleyway is via the Plaza del Flores, at the top, or from the Carrera del Darro at the bottom?"

"Correct."

"…and that there are no houses or properties of any kind on the alleyway, only high walls on either side all the way down?"

"Yes, that's right."

"Then since our witness can confirm that the body was not brought up the alleyway then it would have to have been brought down from Plaza del Flores at the top and that this must have happened between 2.15pm and 2.30pm."

"That would appear to be the only logical conclusion except for one puzzling fact; there is a surveillance camera at the top of the alleyway trained on the plaza. It was installed to protect visitors to the Albacin from the pickpockets and petty thieves that prey on the unsuspecting. I have had the day's contents carefully checked through and although the alleyway was well used in both directions there was nothing to suggest that a body was brought in that way. The forensics team were able to tell us that the murder took place two to three hours before the victim was discovered. The killing must have taken place elsewhere and the body brought to the spot where it was found in the alleyway, otherwise it would have been discovered much sooner.

"What the camera did pick up, however, was that at 2.12pm Pascual Peredes and his dog passed by making their way down the alleyway. Three minutes later at 2.15pm, a man walked into the Plaza del Flores, checked his watch and stood at the top of the entrance to the alleyway. The pictures of him unfortunately are indistinct. At 2.31pm the woman with the red hat appeared at the top of the alleyway. She exchanged a few words with the man and they walked off together out of the plaza in the direction that the man had entered it. The footage then shows Pascual Peredes and his dog appearing at the top of the alleyway hurrying into the plaza. The time was then 2.34pm.

"We need to have a closer look at the spot where the body was found; Fermin and Jaime, I want you to come with me; Edgardo, I need you to organise house-to-house inquiries in Plaza de las Flores. We need to know if any of the residents heard or saw anything suspicious on or before Friday. Mateo, I want you to scan through the camera footage for the past week."

Calle de las Piedras was cordoned off by official tape and entry barred to the public by a uniformed police officer when Chief Inspector Garcia and his two colleagues arrived in Plaza de las Flores. They had parked their car in Calle San Juan de Los Reyes, the nearest point of vehicle access and then walked the short distance to the plaza. Antonio flashed his security card at the uniformed policeman who immediately stepped aside to allow the three men to pass and they made their way down to the point where the body had been discovered. The spot was marked by a white painted cross on the ground, the body itself having been taken to the police morgue. There was a sharp turn in the alleyway just beyond the spot which meant that the bottom of the lane was hidden.

Antonio judged the passageway to be only some four metres wide, with small cobbled stones stretching from wall to wall. The stones were polished by the passage of thousands of shoes over the many years since they had been laid. He estimated the height of the vertical stone walls on either side to be around five metres. "The body must have come over this wall if we are to accept Pascual Peredes' account, and we have no reason to doubt it. There is no other explanation. Also, the body must have been lowered down. If it had simply been dropped then we would have detected much more bruising than was evident."

"The lowest 2m of wall is damp, implying that the ground is higher on the other side," observed Fermin. "The scuff mark at the top edge of the wall could have been made by a rope, but why would anyone go to all this trouble?"

Antonio looked up to the mark. "Whoever did this was keen that the body was quickly found. That would imply that a prominent position was required, but the method of disposal would have to be one that minimised the possibility of being observed in the process. The clear message is that Salón Oscuro don't take kindly to informants or infiltrators and that they were keen to stress the point. We need to see what is on the other side of this wall."

The three officers made their way back up into the plaza. Edgardo was already there speaking to one of the residents at the open door of number 4, Plaza de las Flores. Antonio scanned the plaza. There were twelve properties in total set out as a square with three narrow houses, two stories high on each of the sides. Several of the windows were decorated by red and yellow pots displaying a mass of brightly coloured flowers reflecting the bright sunshine. It was a pleasant, well cared for area. The events of the previous day seemed badly out of place. Apart from the Calle de las Piedras alleyway three other pedestrian passageways led into the plaza. The widest, the one that the officers had walked along after parking their car was on the right. A second was situated between two of the houses on the opposite side, the route taken by the man and the woman with the red hat the day before. The third,

Calle de las Palomas, was on the same side as the Calle de las Piedras opening and, like that passageway, ran steeply down-hill towards Carrera del Darro.

Antonio walked across to Edgardo who had finished talking to the householder. "What have you found out so far?"

"I have only just started sir, but nothing of any real benefit as yet. However, I have been told that an old woman lives at number eleven and that she spends a fair part of the day sat looking out of her window onto the plaza. I still have to speak to her."

"Fermin, I want you to go back down Calle de las Piedras to the position where the body was found. Jaime, come with me." Antonio and Jaime made their way down the alleyway that ran parallel to Calle de las Piedras. This passage way was narrower and the two officers walked in single file with the Chief Inspector in the lead. A steep bank ran up the right-hand side to a high wooden fence. "This must be about opposite the spot, Jaime." The two officers climbed the four weathered steps that led up to a wooden gate. There was no lock on the gate and Antonio pushed it open. Inside was an un-kept yard randomly strewn with discarded metal, tiles and bricks. A dilapidated single storey shed with part of the roof missing stood in one corner. On the far side was a wall no more than one meter high. The two officers crossed to the wall and looked over. Immediately below them was Fermin. He gazed up at his colleagues. "Thanks Fermin, make your way round to us," Antonio ordered and turning to Jaime, "See how the moss on the coping stones is polished flat. The body must have been slid over here and lowered down into Calle de las Piedras. If that is the case then the rope supporting the body must have been untied after it came to rest on the alleyway below. That must have been done by the woman in the red hat."

Antonio turned and made his way towards the shed followed by Jaime. There was no entrance on this front face of the building so they cautiously began to make their way around to the back, stumbling on the uneven ground. The whole building was in a poor state of repair. The windows were boarded up and the glass that had at one time been in the frames, broken and scattered about.

———————

In the Plaza Officer Edgardo was continuing his house-to-house questioning and he approached number 11. Like the others in the plaza, the house was painted white and there was an abundance of flowering pots on the ledges of the downstairs windows. The shutters to the upstairs windows were tightly closed, except for one which had a small railed balcony attached. The door from the balcony to the house was open and on it, facing out towards the plaza, was an empty chair. Edgardo knocked loudly on the front door which was opened almost immediately by a woman. She looked to be in her mid-forties and at her side was a dark-haired boy of about seven or eight. Edgardo showed his police card. "I am speaking to everyone in the plaza in connection with an incident that took place yesterday afternoon. Could I ask you who lives here?"

"Myself, my husband, our two young boys and my elderly mother."

"Did you notice anything unusual in the last few days, any strangers or anyone acting suspiciously?"

The woman thought for a few moments, shrugged her shoulders and replied, "There are always strangers, visitors to the city, passing through the plaza either on their way down to the Carrera del Darro or up in to the Albacin. Nothing unusual that I can think of."

"Would you mind if I spoke to the others in the house?"

"My husband is at work and mother is the only other adult. She is old and gets very confused at times."

"I would like to speak to her anyway if that is possible. It won't take long and I promise not to tire her," Edgardo added.

The woman disappeared into the house but the young boy stood at door way and looked up suspiciously at the uniformed officer. "What's your name young man?" Edgardo asked in a friendly tone. The young boy did not answer but continued to stare up at Edgardo. Then suddenly he turned and ran into the house after his mother. Edgardo idly looked at his watch, checking the time and turned to look at the plaza. It was clear to him that the balcony above must provide an ideal vantage point to watch the comings and goings in plaza. From it there must also be a clear view of the entrances to both Calle de las Piedras and Calle de las Palomas. Eventually the woman returned to the door, this time without the young boy. "My mother is sleeping at the moment. Could you come back in one hour?"

"Of course," Edgardo replied politely and turned to go.

"Please remember that she is elderly, she has a poor concept of time and often speaks of things that happened long ago but, in her mind, she imagines that they took place recently," she called after him.

"I understand."

"I just don't want you to put her under any pressure, she is not strong."

Edgardo nodded, "I will just listen to her. If she remembers seeing anything that might be of use to us, then that would be helpful but you can be assured that I will not take long and of course you will be there. I will go by what you say," and then he added, "Could I just have your names for my notes, it's just routine?"

———

Back at the rear of the derelict shed Antonio and Jaime had been joined by Fermin. The heavy wooden door in front of them was off its hinges and, as instructed by the Chief Inspector, the two junior officers lifted and slid it to one side. Peering inside the first impression that the officers had was of a damp, dirty and virtually empty room. Although the windows were boarded up but light shone through the holes in the ceiling so they could see quite clearly. Antonio was first to step inside. He turned his head towards his two colleagues and instructed, "Take care not to touch or disturb anything. We are only here for an initial look."

"I don't think that this place has been used for many years," Fermin suggested.

Antonio looked at the bare walls. The only furniture was in a corner of the room and consisted of an old, deeply scored table and two stools, both with flaking paintwork. "You may be right." They crossed the room to look more closely at the table and chairs. "Don't you think that it is odd though that everywhere in the room is covered in a thick layer of dust but this table is perfectly clear? It looks to me like it has been cleaned recently. And this area of the floor, close to the wall between here and the door is also dust free, in contrast to where we have walked. Just look at the footprints that we have left."

# 15

## AMALIA

Edgardo had finished the rest of his enquires in Plaza de las Flores hearing nothing of any importance to report to the Chief Inspector. He looked at his watch and noted that it been over an hour since he had visited number 11. It was time to return. He knocked loudly on the door and it was opened almost immediately by the woman that he had met before. "Would it be convenient to have a word with your mother now?" he enquired.

"She is in the kitchen. I have spoken to her and she is expecting you, but remember that you promised that this would not take long," and with that she turned and walked into the hallway. Edgardo followed. The kitchen was entered directly off the hallway. The old lady was sitting in a chair in the corner with a heavy grey blanket wrapped tightly around her.

"My name is Edgardo and I am an officer with the Granada police. I expect that your daughter has told you why I would like to speak to you Madam …"

"You can call me Amalia, everyone does, and yes, my daughter, Maria, told me that you were coming, but I fear that I will not be able to help you much."

Edgardo took a few moments to reply. His police training had taught him how to quickly form an initial impression. Amalia was in her eighties. Her hair was long and grey but well-groomed and her skin was deeply wrinkled by many years in the sun. Edgardo could imagine that Amalia would have been a beautiful woman in her youth. Despite her advanced years she was alert and her sharp blue eyes still shone brightly behind her thick spectacles. "You have lived in Granada for many years?" Egardo opened with a general question to settle the old lady and to gauge her responses.

"Yes, since I was a girl. My family were originally from Lanjarron; myself, my mother, father and my two brothers. We came to the city when my father found work in a steel factory. I met my husband here in Granada and we moved to this house many years ago. When my husband died my daughter and her family moved in to share the house with me. I don't go out much now, but my room has a balcony and I can sit there to pass the time and to remember the old days. My brothers were both killed in the war."

"You must see many interesting things from your balcony?" Edgardo enquired.

Amalia smiled, "I watch the tourists come and go through the plaza."

"They will be en-route to the Alhambra, no doubt," Edgardo casually suggested.

The old lady seemed lost in her thoughts for a moment then commented, "You know that there are two lanes on the other side of the plaza. One is Calle de las Piedras, which leads down to Carrera del Darro and then up to the Alhambra but the other, Calle de las Palomas leads to a dead end. It once was a way into the Convent but that closed long ago. There is now no way through. Some of the tourists would take this lane by mistake. I would try to get their attention to tell them, but they would ignore me and pretend not to hear the old woman. After a few minutes they would return to the plaza and take the correct route. Now I don't bother to shout out. I just watch."

Edgardo listened with interest. "There is nothing else down the lane?"

"My friend Pedro used to have a studio off the lane. He was an artist, a good one, not like these modern artists who paint dobs on their canvases and sell them for hundreds of euros. Pedro painted beautiful scenes of the city, many of the Alhambra. There is little left there now. The studio building has gone and all that is left is an old shed where Pedro stored his paintings."

"That's sad," Edgardo sympathised and then added, "Do many people still make the mistake with the alleyways?"

Amalia was lost in her memories of Pedro and his paintings and did not hear the question properly. "Sorry inspector I did not catch what you asked me."

"I just wondered if you still witnessed individuals getting lost on their way out of the plaza."

"Not so many now. The street maps are better and the young ones are guided by their phones and devices." The expression on Edgardo's face showed his amazement that the old lady knew of such things. "I may be old but I watch television and listen to the news," she added with pride.

"Are there many more questions Inspector. My mother should rest soon." Maria's voice came from behind the Inspector but before Edgardo could reply Amalia prompted, "You have not asked me yet Inspector about the three people who went down Calle de las Palomas and did not return immediately."

———

Antonio and the other two officers made their way back into Calle de las Palomas, the Chief Inspector having already decided that they needed to check out further down the lane. After no more than 50 metres and just around a sharp bend the policemen came to the end of the alleyway. In front of them were the outer walls of the old convent. The door leading in was firmly bolted and from the look of the rusty lock it hadn't been opened for many years.

Antonio's phone rang and he answered it at once, "Yes, Edgardo."

"Chief Inspector, you need to return to the Plaza, I have a witness here with important information." Antonio was met outside the door of number 11 by Edgardo who briefed him on his initial conversation with Amalia. "She is elderly but mentally very sharp. I think that you should hear what she has to say. It would be best if I go back in with you, she seems to find me easy to talk to."

"I can conduct a gentle conversation when I have to," a wry smile crossed Antonio's face, "but if you have her confidence then I agree with you."

"Oh, and one other thing," Edgardo added, "You need to be warned that her daughter will be there and she is quite protective of the old lady. Push things too far and she will terminate the interview."

Amalia was waiting for them in the kitchen. The old lady beamed a smile. It was a long time since she had been paid so much attention. Edgardo introduced Antonio formally to her, "This is Chief Inspector Garcia. He is very interested in what you have to tell us."

"I don't know why," Amalia said with a shrug of her shoulders, "I saw nothing of importance regarding what happened in Calle de las Piedras."

"Perhaps not but I am more interested in what you told Edgardo about the comings and goings in Calle de las Palomas."

The mention of Calle de las Palomas seemed to cause Amalia to be lost in her thoughts again. "Pedro was very handsome," she said, "it was a long time ago, we were both very young."

"Tell me about the person who walked down Calle de las Palomas but did not retrace his steps for some time," prompted Antonio.

"Pedro was a magnificent painter. I spent many hours in his studio admiring his work. The bright colours that he used filled his scenes with life."

"Indeed, but tell me something about the man in Calle de las Palomas on Friday," repeated Antonio rather impatiently.

"Pedro did not make much money from his work. Not as much as he deserved, but he was generous. We dined out regularly in fine restaurants in the city and then danced in the warm summer evenings."

Edgardo was conscious that Antonio was losing patience so he stepped in with a question that he thought might focus Amalia. "What was it about the group of people who went down Calle de las Palomas that caught your attention?"

Amalia looked straight at Edgardo, "One of them looked so like Pedro when he was young, and when they spent so much time in Calle de las Palomas I thought that they must have been visiting the ruins of the old studio. Perhaps he was related to Pedro."

"Can you describe him to me?" Antonio ventured.

"I have an old picture of Pedro which I could let you see. The likeness is quite striking." Turning to her daughter she added, "Maria, fetch the photo from my room for the policemen would you."

Maria returned with the photograph. The picture was proudly preserved in a silver frame although the image was partly faded. It was a picture of Amalia and Pedro together looking straight at the camera and smiling. They looked to be in their twenties. Behind them was a fountain. Antonio recognised the location. The shot was taken in Plaza de Bib-Rambla, close to the cathedral. The Chief Inspector smiled at Amalia, "I would very much like to borrow this if I may." She seemed reluctant to answer so he added, "I know how much this means to you. I promise to take good care of it and return it to you tomorrow."

"It must be important mama. You should let them borrow it. They will return it tomorrow as they say," Maria reassured her mother. Amalia gave a little shrug of her shoulders which the others took to signify hesitant agreement.

Antonio took the photograph, "Thank you. You have been most kind and helpful. Is there anything else that you can tell us before we go and leave you in peace?"

Amalia thought for a moment. "There were three of them, two men and a woman, but the woman and one of the men must have left earlier when I was not paying much attention, because the young man, who looked so much like Pedro was on his own when he left Calle de las Palomas."

"Can you tell me which day this happened, Amalia?"

"I am old; every day is the same to me now. I only know that it was in the morning, before I have my nap. I remember distinctly dreaming of the old days with Pedro."

———

In the house at Mojacar Helen and Manuel sat opposite each other at the dining table, the evening meal that Helen had prepared was on the plates in front of them, the atmosphere decidedly frosty and any conservation that there was between them was strained. Helen eventually broke one of the long periods of silence, "I went to the beach bar this afternoon. The owner told me that you no longer work there."

"Yes, I had to give it up. I have had to spend so much time with my sick aunt in Granada."

"I thought that you told me that your sick aunt was in Cordoba." Manuel did not reply. "Perhaps you should just leave Manuel. I don't feel that I know or can trust you anymore."

"I am sorry Helen, it's just that I have been so busy recently, there has been new developments and responsibilities that I have to deal with away from Mojacar."

Helen's phone rang. The call was from Sam. She walked away from the table, unwilling to share the conversation with Manuel. When she returned Manuel was at the door ready to leave. "Not bad news I hope."

"No, it was just my crazy brother. He says that he is making progress on the code but I fear that he is spending too much time in the sun outside that cave house that he is renting. He has asked me to check on the internet how many times Bobby Moore played for West Ham! I think that he has finally flipped his lid."

# 16

---

**LA TIENDA BARATA**

---

La Tienda Barata, as the name implies, was a shop dedicated to selling cheap items mainly to the tourists who visited the city; fridge magnets, key rings, guide books, tee-shirts and the like. It was situated in a lane off the busy Reyes Catolicos, but the position was less than ideal as most people did not venture off the main street. The proprietor, Diago Alvarez, was standing behind the cluttered counter idly flicking through the pages of the daily paper. The shop door opened and the sound of the bell made him look up. The tall woman who entered wore a smart black trouser suit and down by her side she held a bright red, wide brimmed sun hat, but it was her dark piercing eyes that first caught and demanded his attention. She strode purposefully towards the counter. "Can I help you?" Diago enquired with a smile. The smile was not returned. "I am here on business," she replied curtly. "You are seriously behind on your payments and Hernandez, you will find, is not a patient man, particularly where money is concerned." She took an envelope from her pocket and laid it on the counter. "Details of what you still owe for the services that we have been providing are set out clearly on this invoice."

"But ..." Diago stammered.

"Just see that it is paid and there will be no trouble. You have until 5pm tonight," and with that she turned and left the shop.

Sam Crawford sat patiently outside Chief Inspector Antonio Garcia's office in Granada. He had phoned Antonio only an hour earlier from the cave house with the news that he had broken the code. Although he was currently busy, following up the lead that he had received from Amalia, Antonio was keen to get an update from Sam. After only a few minutes the office door opened and Antonio invited Sam in. There were already three men in the office including Antonio. "Let me introduce you to my colleagues, Fermin Casillas and Jaime Hidalgo. They are working on this case with me." Sam nodded politely to the two officers and took the seat that was offered to him in front of Antonio's desk.

"I believe that you have had a breakthrough with the coded pictures," Antonio began.

"I can tell you what they express but not what they mean," Sam replied.

"Remember that, unlike yourself, we are not mathematicians so please explain your findings in plain language."

"It is actually fairly straightforward," Sam offered. "The key is that the former leader of Salón Oscuro, Danny Thomson, was from the east end of London and from what I have discovered, probably a keen West Ham supporter."

"Go on," prompted the Chief Inspector, intrigued with this development. Sam laid the fifteen pictures down on the table with them facing Antonio.

"The first part was the hardest. Initially I needed to break the set down into smaller groups and then, for each group, find the order that they had to be read in. After a number of fruitless attempts, I tried the following." Sam rearranged the pictures on the desk into two columns as follows:

Column 1: Those with the candle and the fan. There were 7.

Column 2: Those with the candle but no fan. There were 8 of these.

Antonio looked at the two columns, "Fine, but what is so special about this grouping that sets it out from the thousands of other possible groupings?"

"Look closely at each photograph especially at the hour hand on the watch. Each hour, one, two, three etc. is used once and once only in each of these two groups. If my guess that this was in fact the correct grouping, and it strongly suggests that it does, then the order is also defined by rearranging the pictures in each column in the order defined by the hour hand."

"Just give us a second to appreciate that." Antonio turned to the other two officers. "I hope that you are following this."

Sam rearranged the columns on the desk and placed the following card beside them. "This should help."

| Group | Fan<br>p present<br>a absent | Candle<br>p present<br>a absent | Time on watch<br>hours, mins |
|---|---|---|---|
| 1 | p | p | 1,5 |
| 1 | p | p | 2,30 |
| 1 | p | p | 3,45 |
| 1 | p | p | 4,20 |
| 1 | p | p | 5,40 |
| 1 | p | p | 6,20 |
| 1 | p | p | 7,10 |
| 2 | a | p | 1, 5 |
| 2 | a | p | 2,15 |
| 2 | a | p | 3,15 |
| 2 | a | p | 4,30 |
| 2 | a | p | 5,25 |
| 2 | a | p | 6,30 |
| 2 | a | p | 7,20 |
| 2 | a | p | 8,10 |

"The next part was easier. I speculated that the position of the minute hand on the watch represented a letter. The most likely pattern was that the numbers on the dial corresponded to their position in the alphabet. The only problem is of course that there are more than twelve letters in the alphabet. So perhaps you go around the dial twice. That would at least give you twenty-four and suppose that we don't use the last two, Y and Z. I tried several options to find out when the minute hand was indicating one of the first twelve letters and when the second twelve. I found that it was dependent upon the position of the statuette. We now have this." Sam removed the first card and replaced it with the following.

| Group | Fan<br>p present<br>a absent | Candle<br>pL<br>present and lit,<br>pU<br>present and unlit | Time on<br>watch<br>hours, min<br>hand<br>position | Statuette position<br>LS left side<br>RS right side |
|-------|------|------|------|------|
| 1 | p | pL | 1,1 | RS |
| 1 | p | pL | 2,6 | RS |
| 1 | p | pU | 3,9 | RS |
| 1 | p | pU | 4,4 | RS |
| 1 | p | pU | 5,8 | RS |
| 1 | p | pU | 6,4 | RS |
| 1 | p | pU | 7,2 | RS |
| 2 | a | pU | 1, 1 | RS |
| 2 | a | pU | 2,3 | RS |
| 2 | a | pU | 3,3 | RS |
| 2 | a | pU | 4,6 | RS |
| 2 | a | pU | 5,5 | LS |
| 2 | a | pL | 6,6 | RS |
| 2 | a | pL | 7,4 | RS |
| 2 | a | pL | 8,2 | RS |

"So, what do the two groups give us?" The three officers were intrigued.

"I was not quite at a solution yet, but it was becoming interesting. Using this system, the groups read,

Group 1: mrupton

Group 2: moorerpn

These did not seem to make any sense, but then I realised the West Ham connection. The end of group 1 spells out the name of their former home ground, Upton Park, and the beginning of group 2 is the name of their most famous player, Bobby Moore." The officers looked on with increasing interest.

"It seemed sensible to speculate that the first two characters in group 1 and the last three in group 2 could in fact be numbers and not letters. This was confirmed when I looked closer at the candles in the photographs; if lit then we had a letter and when unlit it could indicate something else, perhaps a number. Using this approach leads to the two groupings being, 16upton and moore642. Confirmation that this was correct was obtained when I checked up on a hunch. Bobby Moore played 642 competitive games for West Ham, 544 in the league, 36 cup matches, 49 league cup matches and 13 times in European competitions."

Sam sat back to gauge their reaction. "The only thing is that I have no earthly idea what it all means. I have summarised the result for you." Sam hands the Chief inspector a card with the following notes.

The code:

lit candle – a letter

unlit candle – a number

The minute hand on the watch gives the correct order

The hour hand on the watch in combination with the Dama de Baza gives the following letters.
DDB on left 1A 2B 3C 4D 5E 6F 7G 8H 9I 10J 11K 12L
DDB on right 1M 2N 3O 4P 5Q 6R 7S 8T 9U 10V 11W 12X

The solution:
group 1 (candle and fan) 1-lit,6-lit,9R,4R,8R,3R,2R
= 16upton
group 2 (candle but no fan) 1R,3R,3R,6R,5L,6-lit,4-lit,2-lit
= moore642

Antonio looked at it and thought for a moment before replying, "It looks to me like passwords or a single password of some sort."

"Yes, that makes sense," Sam agreed. "Either 16uptonmoore642 or possibly moore64216upton. If it is a password then it would make sense for Danny Thomson to use something that he would remember, presumably the 16 also had some meaning for him."

Antonio smiled. "Very convincing. Thomson would remember the password easily when needed and the only reason for the picture code was to have it written down as backup but in a secure form, should it become necessary."

He paused then added, "Who else, apart from us four, know that you have deciphered the code?"

"Only my sister Helen."

"Be careful to keep it that way. If this gets out you could be in some danger."

Diago Alvarez put on his jacket. It was 3pm and after having spent the past few hours worrying and contemplating his best course of action, he had phoned his wife telling her to pack a suitcase and be ready to leave. He would be home soon to pick her up; the tone of his voice conveying his anxiety. Diago opened the door of the shop and looked up and down the lane outside. It was deserted. He swiftly stepped through, turned and locked the door behind him. Reyes Catolicos was busy which gave him at least a temporary feeling of security. At the Plaza de Isabel la Catolica he turned left and began to make his way along the Gran Via de Colon crossing over the wide street at the Cathedral. Diago stopped occasionally to look around. He was certain that he was not being followed. At the end of the street Diago turned left into Avenida de la Constitucion, a wide boulevard with a pedestrian zone running down the middle. The entrance to the underground carpark where he had left his car that morning was immediately outside the Jardines del Triunfo. With one last look around to make certain that he was alone, Diago descended the steps to the first underground level. The car park was dimly lit so he briskly made his way past the row of parked vehicles until he reached his own car. Again, he nervously looked around. He was still alone. Diago opened the driver's door of his blue Seat and swiftly sat himself behind the wheel. He had completed the walk from his shop at pace so he gave himself a few moments to catch his breath. Diago turned the ignition key and slowly began to move forward. Immediately a white van from one of the spaces opposite screamed down the car park and stopped across

Diago's parking space completely blocking his exit. Two scruffily dressed men got out and approached Diago's car. "Hernandez wants to see you Señor Alvarez. We have been waiting here to take you to him."

# 1 7

## SACROMONTE

Diago lay uncomfortably on the floor in the white van. His hands had been tightly tied behind his back and the crude blindfold that had been taped around his head dug painfully into his eyes. As the van sped out of the underground car park he rolled about uncontrollably. Diago tried desperately to regain his senses. He had been bundled into the back of the van and as far as he could make out, he was alone in the compartment. The two men were sitting up front exchanging comments but he could not make these out. The sounds of the city drifted in. He could hear the familiar traffic noise broken by the siren from a police car or ambulance as it passed by travelling in the opposite direction.

"Where are they taking me?" Although badly shaken, Diago resolved to keep track of the movement of the van as best he could. It was impossible to determine the direction that he was being taken but he could keep an estimate on the time and on the speed of the van. From the outside sounds it was clear that he was still inside the city. After five or so minutes he was aware that the van was climbing steeply. From this he reasoned that must be travelling in the northern end of the city. Ten minutes later the van began braking heavily and descending. "If the next sharp turn is to the left followed by a twisting steep hill climb then chances are that we have just passed over the west side of the Albacin and are going up into the gypsy quarter, Sacromonte." The next turn was indeed to the left and Diago heard the sharp rasp of the engine as a low gear was selected and the van began to climb again.

The van continued to climb steadily. If this was Sacromonte then, given the time that climb was taking, Diago assumed that they were heading near to the top. The lower end of the single road leading up through the gypsy quarter passed by the caves frequented by the many visitors who came to see the guitar playing and flamenco dancing arranged for their benefit. The upper reaches of the road, however, were virtually deserted. The few caves that existed here were abandoned and in various states of decay with the road itself deteriorating into little more than a rough track. In the back of the van Diago became aware of a change in the surface, adding yet more substance to his speculations.

Eventually the van came to a stop. Diago tensed as he heard the back-door creak open. "Just checking that you are comfortable." The sarcasm was lost on Diago as he felt the blindfold being tightened further and the binding on his hands checked. "This is as far as we can take you. You need to wait here and shortly another driver will take you on the rest of the way." Then without waiting for a reply the door was slammed shut.

The thin walls of the van and the lack of ventilation had made the temperature inside climb steadily adding to Diago's discomfort. Time passed. How long? Diago could only guess. It seemed like hours but in fact was more like half an hour. Exhausted, he had just begun to drift into a state of semi-consciousness when the van door was pulled open again. "Sorry to keep you waiting." Diago recognised the female voice of the woman who had entered his shop. "We have to take these precautions. Hernandez must keep his identity and location secret. He has many enemies. I will take you the rest of the way to meet him."

The van's engine kicked into life and the driver executed a swift three-point turn. Diago was aware that they were now heading back downhill. After a few minutes he was thrown against the side of the van as it made a sharp turn to the left. The speed was now reduced to a crawl as the driver negotiated a route to avoid the worst of the ruts in the uneven surface. Eventually the van came to a standstill and the rear doors were flung open. "We go the rest of the way by foot. I will guide you. Don't try to break my grip of your arm. The way is dangerous and any attempt to escape blindfolded would be futile."

Diago was led forward and he was aware that they were making their way through thick undergrowth as bushes brushed against him and at every step, sticks cracked under his feet. He was vaguely aware of the sound of a stream somewhere in the distance ahead of them. Suddenly Diago felt much cooler. They had moved out of the sun. "Where are we?" His words echoed and it was clear to him that they had passed into a cave. They came to a stop and Diago flinched as the blindfold was ripped from him. He shook his head but was still unable to see about him in the darkness. A heavy door behind him slammed shut and he heard the sound of the key locking it. Diago's hands were still tied behind his back and he stood still giving his eyes time to become accustomed to the dark. Gradually he began to see outlines and faint shapes.

"Welcome to Salón Oscuro Señor Alvarez." The deep voice from somewhere in front of him made Diago jump. "We are both business men and I have a proposition to put to you." Diago remained silent. "You owe me a considerable amount of money so we need to find some way that you can clear this debt." What then seemed like a long period of silence ensued which was finally broken with, "I need you to stock certain items for me in your shop that will be collected from time to time by a few chosen clients of mine. It will be a private arrangement between us and for this I will close off your debt. Of course, if you speak to anyone about this then the deal is closed and you will have to face the consequences."

Diago finally found his voice. "What are these items?"

"That needn't concern you. You will store them in the back room of the shop away from your customers. My clients will make themselves known and you will give the parcels to them when they call on you."

"I want to speak to Danny Thomson. I have always dealt with him in the past"

The reply was swift and angry "He is no longer with us. I am in charge now!"

# 18

## A SIGNIFICANT
## PHONE CALL

Sam Crawford looked out across the valley from the small patio area in front of the Freila cave house. The situation was idyllic. He had been able to spend the last few days relaxing and preparing the talk that he would be giving to the mathematics faculty at Granada University, "Pattern Recognition as an Aid to Code Breaking." The presentation was virtually complete but he still felt that it needed an inspiring ending, something to make the talk more memorable. He was deep in thought when the ring tone on his phone indicated that there was an incoming message. Casually he opened the communication. It was from Chief Inspector Garcia. It read "Dear Sam, the Granada police are very grateful for the excellent assistance that you provided in breaking the Salón Oscura code. Although we do not know its significance yet it would appear to be a password for access to some file that the Salón Oscuro gang, and in particular Hernandez, the present leader, value. In recognition of your efforts on our behalf one of my officers has been liaising with the Italian police in Florence. I didn't mention this to you before now as it was unlikely that this would lead anywhere. However, I have to say that we have now uncovered a possible line of inquiry that might have a bearing on your wife's disappearance. I don't want to raise false hopes but I should say that the information that we have received could be significant. When you get this message give me a ring to arrange a meeting here at my office."

Sam put the phone down on the wall while he gathered his thoughts. Almost immediately it rang. "Hello, Sam Crawford here."

"Hi Sam, it's Helen," his sister's voice was clear. "Just thought that I would give you a call to find out how you are and what you are up to."

"Helen, I have just had a message from the Granada police. They have possible news regarding Carol. I have to phone Chief Inspector Garcia to arrange a meeting."

"What! Please don't build your hopes up too much. You know that you have had disappointments in the past."

"I understand sis, but this seems different somehow."

"Just be careful Sam. Look, the main reason for my call is that I am concerned about the fact that you are in Freila on your own. Even if the gang are unaware that you have broken the code, they could still be trying to find you."

"No one apart from yourself and the Granada police know where I am. Besides I am sure that Salón Oscuro, and Hernandez in particular, will be assuming that the police have me safely out of the area, probably back in the UK."

"Still, I think that I would be happier if you were to come back down to Mojacar."

"I like it here and the peacefulness is helping me prepare my talk to the University."

"Stubborn as usual. In that case I am coming up to you."

"Ok if that's what you want but it would rather cut off your time with your waiter friend, Manuel wouldn't it?" Sam teased.

"I told you already that that particular relationship has cooled somewhat." Helen was not amused.

"Well it is up to you to do what you want. I need to go now Helen. I have to make that call to Chief Inspector Garcia", and with that Sam pressed the end call button on his phone.

Fifteen minutes later Sam was on his way to Granada driving along the A92 motorway with his meeting with Chief Inspector Antonio Garcia arranged. Like most of the motorways in that part of Spain the road was not particularly busy and Sam had to fight the urge to exceed the 120kph limit. In just under the hour he was turning off at junction 253, Viznar, which was the quickest way into the city centre.

––––––––

Diago Alvarez sat quietly behind the counter in his shop. The sign on the door of La Tienda Barata indicated that it was shut. He needed time to gather his thoughts. Since the exchange at Salón Oscuro all that he could remember was being thrown from the van, back in the underground carpark where he had first been picked up. His head still hurt from the blow that had knocked him out before the journey down the hill.

As his head gradually cleared Diago became aware that someone was moving about in small store room at the back of the shop. Alarmed he called out "Who's there?" The store room door swung open. Framed by the door way was a tall, scruffily dressed individual. He had long black greasy hair and a dirty un-kept beard. Although he was over-weight, he looked strong. His narrow eyes looked back at Diago. "I am Sergio, your new assistant."

"I have no need for a new assistant," ventured Diago.

"If you have any problem regarding this arrangement then I suggest that you take it up with Señor Hernandez."

"You work for Hernandez?" Diago felt a cold chill envelop his body. "What is it that you do for him?"

"Anything that he asks me to. Sometimes I have to hurt people."

———

Sam was ushered into Chief Inspector Garcia's office. The police officer extended his hand in welcome, "Good to see you Sam, please take a seat."

"You have word of my wife?" Sam was keen to dispense

with formalities and to hear what the police in Italy had discovered.

Antonio was acutely aware of Sam's emotional dilemma and began the account without delay. "The story that I am about tell you has only just come to light and is in connection with a recent arrest made by the Italian police in Florence. Let me tell you what we know before you ask me any questions." Sam nodded and the Chief Inspector continued. "On the day of your wife's disappearance there was an armed raid on an expensive jewellery shop in the centre of Florence. The thieves managed to escape and until recently the case remained unsolved. However, early this week the Italian police made an arrest in connection with a completely separate incident and as part of the interrogation of the suspect he confessed to being part of former raid on the jewellery shop. Let's call him Mr. X"

"I can't see what this has to do with Carol's disappearance."

"Have patience, I am coming to that. Mr. X was obviously troubled by the events that followed, which he had been forced to keep to himself and now that he had begun to tell his story. It was plain to the officers present that he was relieved to get things finally off his chest.

"The raid had apparently gone to plan except for one small detail; there was a witness who saw the gang leave the shop. One rash member of the gang had removed the mask covering his face before getting into the getaway van and in full sight of the witness. Then, whether a deliberate act or accident we will never know, but in any case, the van swerved, mounting the pavement knocking the witness heavily against a wall. In the ensuing panic the van stopped and she was bundled into the back before it made off at speed."

"You said, she. You believe this was Carol?"

"Not so fast, there is more. Let me continue. The gang were based in Pisa not Florence and on their way back to Pisa there was heated discussion as to what they should do with the witness. She was obviously badly hurt having suffered a serious head knock."

Sam was unable to keep silent any longer, "Did she recover, where is she now?"

"Please remember that we are not sure if this woman is your wife, Carol. I can only pass on to you what I have been told."

"It's her, it has to be." Sam stood up from his chair. "I have to see her."

"It is likely that you will find the next part of this story upsetting, so please try to stay as calm as possible and bear with me 'til I finish.

"On the way back to Pisa the gang argued about what to do with the witness. The woman was certainly seriously hurt and lay unconscious in the back of the van. The original arrangement had been that the gang would split up and make their own separate ways back into the town, with the intention of meeting up again a few days later. The witness had complicated the plan. It was decided that she had to be eliminated and the person who had to carry out the act was the one foolish enough to remove his mask in the first place, Mr. X. Accordingly both he and the witness left the van on a quiet stretch of country road about five miles outside of Pisa. She was still unconscious and he carried her into the wood at the side of the road. The instruction was that he was to do away with the witness, dispose of the body in the wood and then make his own way to Pisa."

Antonio could see the alarm in Sam's eyes so quickly added, "The act was never carried out. Just bear with me a few moments more. According to the account given to the Florence police by Mr. X, he carried the unconscious witness into the woods but was unwilling to carry out the gang's orders. He could see that the woman required urgent medical assistance and knowing the area well he carried her through the woods and across a field to the outer wall of a strict order convent, il Convento delle Sorelle Povere. He laid the witness down at a door in the wall, rang the bell and quickly left the scene.

"We need to speculate on what happened next. It would be fair to assume that the nuns took her in and attended as best they could to her injuries."

"And she must still be there," Sam added, again getting to his feet.

"Remember that we don't know for certain that this woman is your wife, Carol, but there is more. The Italian police have made enquiries at il Convento delle Sorelle Povere and have confirmed that they did take in an injured woman and the date coincides with that when your wife disappeared. She is in their care and is now physically well. However due probably to the severe blow that she had to the head and the traumatic effect of the events on the day that she was injured, she has no memory of anything prior to her time at the convent."

"It's Carol, it has to be!" Sam was beside himself. "I must go now to this convent."

"Of course, that will be arranged, but first I would like you to look at this photograph that was given to us by an old lady who lives in Plaza de las Flores, Granada. Does the picture remind you of anyone?"

Sam took the picture from Antonio and turned it over to look closely at it. "Yes, it does, but I don't quite understand …"

"It may mean nothing. It just ties in with a specific line of our investigations."

# 19

## CONVENTO DELLE
## SORELLE POVERE

Sam nervously typed Helen's numbers into his phone. There was no answer. He hung up and typed the following text, "Helen, it's me. I need you here immediately. I'm at the cave house in Freila. You have to come with me to Italy tomorrow. I will explain everything when you arrive. Please get back to me once you receive this message."

Sam nervously paced the small patio outside the cave house, holding tightly onto his cell phone, willing it to ring. When it eventually did, it made him jump and the phone dropped heavily on to the concrete floor of the patio. "Shit." He picked it up. It was scratched but seemed otherwise intact and was still ringing and he pressed the receive button.

"What's the panic Sam?"

"Helen, I think I know where Carol is. I am going to see her tomorrow in Italy. The Granada police have made all the necessary arrangements and I need you to come with me."

"Slow down Sam, of course I will come, but please don't build your hopes up too much. I don't want to see you get hurt if this turns out to be a false lead." After a short pause, Helen continued, "I was about to phone you in any case. Manuel has been pestering me to arrange a meeting with you to discuss a business proposition."

"Manuel Fuentes, the waiter from the beach bar, I thought he was a thing of the past and that my location was to be kept secret for the time being."

"He is and it is."

"That can wait, just come up here on your own, preferably tonight."

At eight thirty in the evening Sam heard the sound of Helen's car coming along the narrow lane above. She quickly parked and began to walk down the narrow pathway leading down to the cave house. Sam was already out to meet her. "It must be her! everything fits."

"Just slow down a bit Sam. Let me at least get indoors and then you can tell me more."

Once inside Sam recounted what Antonio had told him. "It must be Carol. The dates, the circumstances, it all makes sense. We need to go to the convent tomorrow. The Granada police have arranged for us to be met at Florence airport and taken there."

"I agree Sam that it could possibly be Carol. But let's not jump to any conclusions. It may not be." Helen hesitated for a moment then added, "The police did say that the woman at the convent was still suffering from the injuries that she sustained." A further pause then, "You are prepared for that, aren't you Sam?"

The drive from Florence airport to il Convento delle Sorelle Povere seemed, at least to Sam, to take an age. The driver assigned to them spoke only a little English and neither Sam nor Helen knew much Italian. Eventually the car slowed down and the driver turned off from the main road and they started to make their way along a narrow lane. The driver made some comment to Sam which he couldn't fully understand but it seemed that he could have been telling them that it was not far to go now. Sam tensed as the convent came into sight and Helen took hold of his arm. "Are you ok Sam?" Sam nodded weakly. The driver stopped the car and got out. He rang the bell and then returned to the car. "I wait here for you. One of the sisters take you inside." Sam and Helen got out of the car and nervously went over to the gate." Helen could see the strain in her brother's face. "Are you sure you want me to come with you? You may want to go the rest of the way on your own."

"I need you to come with me Helen. This is not easy for me."

The gate creaked open and a young nun dressed in a black cloak and hood beckoned for them to come in. "I'm Sam Crawford and this is my sister Helen." The nun did not reply but instead put a finger across her mouth and silently indicated a shush. "Some of the order must have taken a vow of silence," Sam said to Helen. "I hope that there is someone here that we can talk to." The nun led them across the grass from the gate to the door of the convent. The place was old and looked foreboding. Looking around, they could see no sign of life in the grounds. All was still and quiet adding to the earie atmosphere of the place. The young nun pushed the door open and indicated that they should go inside. She followed them in and then crossed the hall to where two old wooden stools had been placed. The nun indicated that they should sit here and when they did, she turned and made off through a door at the far side of the hall. "What now?" Sam ventured.

"We obviously wait here," Helen suggested. "At least they have provided us with something to sit on. I get the impression that they don't go big on luxuries here."

The hall was dark and gloomy. Apart from the two stools the floor was bare. Pictures of the crucifixion hung on the walls and in a small alcove opposite was a figurine of a woman kneeling, with her head bowed and her hands together obviously deep in prayer. Eventually the door through which the young nun had passed opened again and a similarly dressed, but much older nun approached them. "I am sister Anna," she said and smiled at them reassuringly. Please don't try to speak to any of the nuns. Most of them have taken a vow of silence as part of their devotions. Only myself and a few others are privileged to speak. We have very little dealings with the world outside these walls but we are not completely self-sufficient and it is necessary for the well-being of our convent that there is some contact, if a little restricted." Sam and Helen nodded that they understood. Both of them finding it difficult to respond appropriately. "I believe that you have come to visit one of our friends who is in our care. We don't know her name but we have called her Mary. I understand that you are aware of the circumstances surrounding how she end up here and also know that she remembers nothing prior to her arrival. Mary is physically well but relies heavily on the support that we have been able to offer her."

"I think she may be my wife, Carol Crawford."

"We must be very careful Mr. Crawford, Mary's condition is very delicate. I suggest that you proceed with caution. We all here want what is best for her, as I am sure you do. She may or may not be your wife Carol. Mary has been told to expect visitors today but nothing else. If you are ready, we will go now to see her."

———

It was dark and quiet outside the cave house in Freila. The street lights in the narrow roadway above cast only a dim light on the patio below. He gave quick look over his shoulder to confirm that no one was around and then inserted the key into the door lock. He pushed the heavy metal door open. It was stiffer than he imagined that it would be. Stepping inside and silently closing the door behind him he took a small torch from his pocket and shone it around the room. He carefully traced the beam around the white walls as the reflected light showed up a small area at a time. The room was pretty much as he had imagined it would be. Eventually the beam settled on a small wooden cabinet in one corner. This, he decided, was the most obvious place to start his search. The cabinet had a flat top where a writing pad, some pens and a calculator were neatly arranged. There was a single drawer with storage shelves below. The drawer was not locked and slid out from the cabinet easily. Shining his torch around the room he was able to see the position of the dining table on the wall near the entrance door. Its surface was clear except for some cork table mats. These were quickly pushed to one side and the contents of the drawer emptied onto the table. He separated the items out. There was a map of Andalucia, an assortment of guide books including Granada, Seville and Cordoba and receipts for water and electricity payments; clearly not what he was looking for. He returned to the cabinet. On the storage shelves were three black folders. This, he decided looked more promising. The folders were laid out on the table. Each had a label on the outside cover. The first read "Lecture notes for Granada talk", the second simply "Miscellaneous" and the third "Coding Notes". This third folder was more what he was looking for. Excitedly he laid it on the table and began to flick through the contents.

Almost immediately all the lights in the cave came on and the two-bedroom doors swung open. An armed police officer immerged from one and Chief Inspector Antonio Garcia from the other. "Found what you are looking for senior Fuentes? I think not. The code notes that you are after are safely in my office in Granada."

Manuel Fuentes turned around in shock, dropping the folder back onto the table, "But…"

"We have had our eye on you for some time now. We had a lucky break with an old woman in Granada who saw you in Calle de las Palomas and thought that you looked like a friend of hers from many years ago. The likeness to a photograph that she kept is quite striking. Pure chance of course, we have not been able to establish any connection." The Chief Inspector paused for a few seconds to see if Manuel would reply. He did not, so Antonio continued, "But our suspicions were raised far earlier than that. You see, although any one from the University in Granada would have known about the travel arrangements of Dr. Crawford only someone with a bit more knowledge could possibly have known about the significance of the Dama de Baza statuette to the Crawfords. I suspect that Helen, Sam Crawford's sister may have innocently have mentioned that to you in the past."

"Look, I only work for Salón Oscuro, I have had nothing to do with the killings. You have got to believe me. The gang has become more violent since Hernandez took over from Danny Thomson and I have been trying to get out."

"I am inclined to believe you señor Fuentes." Antonio looked sternly at Manuel and added pointedly, "It would be in your best interests to help us find Hernandez."

# 2 0

## CAROL?

Sister Anna led Sam and Helen along a dimly lit passageway deep into the centre of the convent. At the end of the passageway was a heavy door which she swung open. They stepped through and out into a sunlight central patio area. The sweet smell of flowers filled the air and in one corner there was a small fountain who's gently running water broke the silence of the scene. It was a peaceful, pleasant spot. Sam glanced around the patio. There were two doors on each of the four surrounding walls, each with a small window to their left. Sister Anna pointed to one of the doors. "Mary has her room here. Let me go in first to make sure that she is ready to meet you."

The nun crossed over to the room, placed her ear

close to the wooden door and knocked gently. Sam and Helen watched as Sister Anna opened the door slightly and slipped inside. She closed the door quietly behind her and Sam and Helen were again alone. Sam gazed around the patio and up the surrounding stone walls. Above the ground floor where they stood was a second floor. The rooms on this level were set back slightly from a narrow walkway that ran all the way around. Above that he could see the blue sky and could just make out the curved tiles which formed the roof of the building. Sam turned to Helen, "It's very peaceful here, an ideal spot for Carol to recuperate."

"Don't let yourself get too far ahead Sam. Remember we are not sure that we are going to find this to be Carol."

The door through which Sister Anna had passed opened and with a small wave of the hand the nun beckoned them to enter. Sam walked swiftly to the door. Helen was immediately behind him. Sam turned to his sister, "I need this to be Carol."

"I know you do," she replied and they stepped inside.

Sister Anna was standing at the far side of the small, sparsely furnished room. Against one wall was a bed, on another, a wooden desk with a candle and a bible. Sitting on a stool beside the nun, but facing the wall was the person that they had come to see. Sister Anna placed her hand on the woman's shoulder and quietly said to her, "Your visitors are here Mary, turn around and you will see them."

Slowly the woman turned until she was facing them. Sam saw immediately that it was Carol. Unable to restrain himself he rushed forward and shouted out, "Carol." Carol recoiled and nervously turned back to face the wall causing Sam to stop in his tracks. He looked to the nun, "I am sorry, I didn't mean to alarm anyone but this is my wife Carol, she has been missing for so long." He turned to his sister, "It is her isn't it?"

"Yes Sam, it is," she confirmed.

Sister Anna looked at them both, "You must remember what Mary has been through. She obviously doesn't recognise you. You will need to be careful not to upset the small progress that she has made since she came to us."

"Of course," Sam replied adding, "I am just so glad to see her."

"I understand but for the moment I think it best if you just leave and let things take their time."

"I only want what's best for Carol. I must come back to see her later."

"Leave it for a day or two and we shall see."

Carol was facing the wall again. Sam took the Dama de Baza statuette from his pocket and placed it upon the table. "I want her to have something of her own if that's ok."

Sister Anna smiled, "Yes, I am sure that would be good, but now I must insist that you go. Don't worry, your wife is being well looked after here."

# 21

## THE INTERROGATION

Diago Alvarez stood outside his shop. He had been walking about in the streets surrounding La Tienda Barata for the past hour trying to decide what he should do. Going to the police could cause difficulties for him and his family. He was fully aware, from what he had read in the papers, that Salón Oscuro had increasingly turned to violence over the past few years but still he felt it his duty to provide the Granada police with vital information regarding the location of the cave in Sacromonte that he had been taken to. He was still undecided when he entered the shop. The shop was quiet, much as he had left it, but unusually there was no sign of Sergio. Since his arrival Sergio had set up permanent residence in the shop and, as far as Diago was aware, never left it. "Strict orders from Hernandez," Diago recalled him saying.

Diago went into the back shop. Still no sign of Sergio and, to his added surprise, nor was there any sign of the few belongings that usually lay scattered on the floor. Evidently Sergio had left and it must have been recently as he was still in the shop when Diago had gone out about an hour before. Diago went back into the front shop. Going behind the counter he instinctively opened the till to check its contents. It was empty and there had been about 1,500 euros in there earlier. "It looks like he left in a hurry and is unlikely to be returning soon." With the immediate pressure of Sergio's constant attention lifted, Diago's mind was made up. "Now is the time for me to go to the police."

———

Chief Inspector Antonio Ferrer Garcia looked across the table in the interview room at Manuel Fuentes and his lawyer Marcos Lopez. "You have agreed to help us in our enquiries into the murders of Danny Thomson and police officer Paco Bosque. I advise you to answer my questions truthfully."

"My client is not in any way connected with these murders. He admits to have been a minor member of the Salón Oscuro gang and that is all. He is willing to assist you but I am afraid that there is little of any consequence that he has knowledge of."

Antonio gave the lawyer dark look. "I will be the judge of that." He switched on the recording device and began, "Interview commenced at 18.30 hours; those present,

Chief Inspector Antonio Ferrer Garci and officer Fermin Casillas of the Granada Police Department, Manuel Fuentes and Abogado, Marcos Lopez," and then turning to Manuel, "You are Manuel Fuentes, a waiter in the beach bar El Arbol Verde in Mojacar?"

"Yes"

"How long have you worked there?"

"I left recently but worked there, part time, for about three years."

"Why did you leave?"

"I was asked to leave."

"Why?"

"The owner thought that I was taking too much time off."

Antonio paused for a moment, fixed Manuel with a stare and then said, "You were becoming more deeply involved with the Salón Oscuro gang." It was delivered more as a statement than a question. Manuel Fuentes looked over at Marcos Lopez who shook his head indicating that he should not answer. Manuel remained silent. "Describe to me what you know of the events leading up to the murder of the former leader of the gang, Danny Thomson."

"I can't help you. I was working in the Arbol Verde beach bar in Mojacar that afternoon and evening."

"We will check that out." After a short pause, "Let us turn then to the case of police officer Paco Bosque. We have evidence that places you at the scene of the crime around the time of his murder."

Fuentes looked alarmed, "No, I took Paco to the old outbuilding in Calle de las Palomas and then left. Certain

Salón Oscuro members suspected that he was connected with the police in some way, probably as an informant, and I thought that the plan was simply to frighten him and to leave him there. He was unaware of our suspicions. We tied him up but otherwise he was unhurt when I left."

"You say, "We," who else was with you?"

Fuentes looked over at his lawyer but he saw no reaction so he answered, "Frieda Weber."

"Tell me more about Frieda Weber."

"I know very little about her, except that she came originally from Germany, somewhere near Munich and now lives in Córdoba. She joined Salón Oscuro when Hernandez took over."

The Chief Inspector glanced towards officer Fermin Casillas and directed his comment, "The person that we know as the woman in the red hat?"

Antonio changed his approach, "How do you know Helen Crawford?"

"We were friends."

"When did you discover that her brother was Dr. Samuel Crawford, a prominent mathematician, specialising in coding?"

"Helen told me soon after we first met. It just came out in general conversation. I thought nothing much about it at the time."

"How did Hernadez find out about Sam Crawford and his skill in coding?"

"I have never met Hernandez so I have no idea. Some other member of Salón Oscuro must have passed the information on."

Antonio paused for a moment then continued, "Tell me what you do know of the mysterious Hernandez."

"Nothing. As far as I know only one person has contact with him."

"And who is that?"

Fuentes shifted uneasily on his seat and looked over at his lawyer for further guidance. "Frieda Weber."

"My client is not prepared to answer any further questions," interjected Marcos Lopez.

The Chief Inspector rose abruptly to his feet and, with anger in his voice, stated, "Then this interview is terminated."

———

Diago Alvarez sat anxiously in the waiting room outside Chief Inspector Garcia's office. He had been shown there on his arrival at the police station by a duty officer. He was told that the Chief Inspector was carrying out an important interview and had given strict orders not to be disturbed. Diago had told the duty officer that he had significant information but would only pass this on directly to the Chief Inspector.

The office door swung open and Manuel Fuentes and his lawyer came through, out into the waiting room. Manuel instantly caught sight of Diago sitting in the seat in the corner and gave out an audible gasp. He caught the arm of his lawyer, "I must speak to the Chief Inspector again immediately." Without waiting for a response, he turned abruptly and went back into the office.

Antonio was collecting his papers together as Manuel re-entered the office. Manuel approached and quickly sitting back down at the interview table declared, "I want to speak further," then added cautiously, "Why is Diago Alvarez waiting outside?"

Although Antonio was unaware of who Diago Alvarez was, or why he might be waiting to see him, he seized the initiative and speculated, "He has information that he wishes to share with me." Manuel Fuentes visibly froze, his eyes seemed to search the ceiling for inspiration. After a moment's hesitation he went on, "I think that I can help you further with your search for Hernandez."

Marcos Lopez came back into the room and abruptly indicated to Fuentes, "I advise you to say no more."

"The police know about the location in Sacromonte. I am not going to take the rap for Hernandez."

Although the Chief Inspector was mystified by the remark, he grabbed the opportunity to take advantage of the situation and switched the recording device back on. With a slight inclination of the hand, he indicated that Manuel should continue, "Interview with Manuel Fuentes recommenced at 19.05, also present are Chief Inspector Antonio Ferrer Garci, Fermin Casillas and Abogado, Marcos Lopez."

"I don't know who the real Hernandez is. I'm not sure that anyone in Salón Oscuro does, except perhaps one, Frieda Weber." He stopped to gather his thoughts. Antonio patiently waited and eventually Manuel went on, "Occasionally, under orders I have pretended to be Hernandez to frighten our clients." Antonio thought that the use of "clients" was misplaced but he did not want to break Manuel's flow.

"Go on."

"Hernandez is a dangerous man. I know that he lives alone somewhere in Córdoba and seldom leaves there. When he took over Salón Oscuro it was Frieda Weber who informed us and she became the link between him and our operations here in Granada. Any orders from Hernandez are relayed through Frieda Weber. I don't doubt that Hernandez killed Danny Thomson and probably Paco Bosque as well."

"Someone in Salón Oscuro must have met him when he took over."

"No, Danny Thomson was killed when he was out on his own in the city. Two days later Frieda Weber, turned up at Sacromonte and announced that Hernandez had taken over as leader and that she would be relaying his instructions."

"Where will I find Frieda Weber?"

"I don't know exactly. As I told you earlier, somewhere in Córdoba. I have told you all that I can."

Antonio turned towards the recording device, "Interview terminated at 19.20." He switched the recorder off and then, to Fuentes and his lawyer, "That's all for the moment but I will need to speak to you further later. Fermin, take Fuentes back to the cells then come back here." Fuentes and his lawyer were escorted out of the room. Almost immediately the Duty officer poked his head round the office door, "I have a gentleman outside who has been waiting to speak to you. His name is Diago

Alvarez, he owns a shop called La Tienda Barata, near to the Cathedral."

"Show him in."

Diago entered the office. He was obviously agitated and Antonio tried to put him at his ease. "Please sit-down Señor Alvarez. It is good of you to come. My assistant, officer Fermin Casillas, will be with us soon and you can tell us both what you have to say. Meanwhile try to relax."

# 2 2

## CÓRDOBA

Frieda Weber looked out of the window of her small, two room flat in Córdoba, down into the narrow, cobbled lane below. The lane led off from the Calle de Rey Heredia, a popular route taken by tourists on the way to and from the Mezquita and the Alcazar when exploring deeper into the old part of the city. From the window she could see a group of visitors, deep in conversation, making their way down the lane and, going in the opposite direction, a family of six, the mother and father trying their best to keep the children in order. Frieda moved away from the window and back into the sparsely furnished room that served as her main living quarters. In one corner was a round wooden table with two chairs where she sat to eat meals. Against the wall opposite to the window were two shabby, unmatched chairs. The room was devoid of any ornaments or pictures and gave the overall impression that it was only being used as temporary accommodation. There were two doors in the room. One led out directly to the communal staircase and the other to the bedroom which in turn led to the bathroom. To one side of the main door was a cat basket. As usual Frieda's black cat was asleep in the basket. When Frieda had taken over rental of the flat the cat had followed her in off the lane and had decided to take up residence with her. Frieda maintained that she had not adopted the cat, rather that the cat had adopted her.

Frieda sat down on one of the chairs. She needed time to decide what to do next. Since the arrest of Manuel Fuentes, the remaining gang members had decided to split up and to go their separate ways. They were never a close-knit group, preferring to maintain a discreet distance, and now that the Granada police were sure to be following up any leads that they had, it was more important than ever to break any way of connecting one to the other. She felt reasonably secure in her flat in Córdoba, so provided that she kept a low profile for the next week or two, she felt that things should blow over and then she could make further plans. Meanwhile it was easy to blend in with the tourists in the old quarters of the city and besides there was still business to conclude in Córdoba.

Frieda looked at her watch. It was 7.30am and her routine meeting was at 8.00am. She looked out of the window onto the lane below. It was a fine morning. In a few hours the temperature would be rising steadily towards its peak for this time of year of 35 degrees, but at the moment it would be pleasantly warm outside. She put on her red sun hat and opened the door of her flat, locked it, and made her way down into the lane. It was still early so the narrow streets were empty. She turned into Calle Cardenal Hererro, where, in contrast, the city was awake and bustling with life. She looked across the street towards the high stone walls that enclosed the Mezquita and its grounds. Through the Torre Campanario arch she could see into the Patio de las Naranjos, a tree lined grove that marked the entrance to the Mezquita and the Catedral de Córdoba. A number of tourists were already milling about in the grove waiting for the famous mosque and cathedral to open. They were obviously aware that the first hour was free to visitors with paid entrance beginning for those arriving after 10am. The wall of the Mezquita occupied one side of the narrow, cobbled streets that circled the mosque, on the other side was range of tourist shops, cafes and restaurants. The shops were narrow and their shelves heaving with colourful tourist gifts. Between the shops narrow lanes led back through patio areas to individual restaurants and hotels. Frieda made her way up one of the lanes to the large patio area of the restaurant that she frequented. Spread around the patio were a number of tables, many of them set for breakfast and already occupied. The high surrounding walls were liberally decorated with colourful ceramic pots and drapes. Small birds flew above and swooped down, picking up scraps from the ground and from any of the empty tables. In the centre of the patio area was a small fountain with water trickling over its sides and down into a channel which flowed to a drain near one of the walls. Frieda glanced across to the far side of the patio and then briskly stepped over to the table where the meeting always took place. She sat down beside the single occupant.

"Hello Frieda," he said, neatly folding the newspaper that he had been reading, placing it on the table between them, "I have ordered our usual coffees."

# 2 3

SALÓN OSCURO,
SACRAMONTE

Fermin Casillas knocked on Antonio's office door, opened it slightly and tentatively looked in. "You wanted to see me Chief Inspector?"

"Yes, come in Fermin." Antonio was sitting at his desk and he motioned, with a wave of his hand, for Fermin to take a seat. "We need to move quickly on the leads that we have on Salón Oscuro and, in particular, on Hernandez." Fermin nodded in agreement. He knew from experience that it was best simply to listen to the Chief Inspector on occasions such as this. "Manuel Fuentes has given us a good description of Frieda Weber and she is our best lead to Hernandez himself. He also told us that she has a flat somewhere in the old part of Córdoba and that she is German. She may not stay there for much longer, of course, now that the gang have split. The police in Córdoba are working with us and are trying to determine her exact whereabouts. I have told them that she should not be approached, should they find her. We need her followed to lead us to Hernandez. If they do make contact, then I intend to go to Córdoba and I want you and Jaime Hidalgo to come with me." Fermin nodded again. "Meanwhile Diago Alvarez will take us to the spot in Sacramonte that he believes to be where he met the person that he thought was Hernandez. We now know, of course, that that person was in fact Manuel Fuentes who we have in custody, posing as Hernandez in order to put pressure on Diago."

The traffic was particularly heavy as the three officers and a rather apprehensive Diago Alvarez, drove through the congested city streets. Fermin was at the wheel, Antonio opposite him in the front seat, Jaime was in the back with Diago. Fermin flicked the switch that activated the siren and immediately the cars in front gave way allowing the police car to make better progress. Pedestrians on the crowded pavements turned to watch as Fermin expertly weaved his way through the gaps left by the other cars. After about ten minutes the police car turned left to begin its steep climb up into the Sacramonte district. Antonio turned around to face Diago. "Slow down now Fermin and let Diago gather his recollection of the journey that he took," and then to Diago, "is this about the speed that you were travelling at?"

Diago looked anxiously out of the window. "More or less," he said but without a great deal of conviction. After a further five or six minutes he added, "I think that this is about as far as we came in the van with the first driver. We stopped about now and after some time the woman took over, turned the van around and headed back down the hill. This only took a few minutes. The van was parked and then the woman and I went off by foot to the left into the scrub. I don't think that it was a proper path as it felt very uneven under foot." Fermin did a three-point turn and headed back down-hill stopping when Diago felt that he had repeated the journey as well as he could recollect.

The bushes and scrub at the side of the road at this point were dense and the ground fell away steeply to the river far below them. The chief inspector stepped out of the car and looked around. "It could take some time to check this area out, we will need some help." He took out his phone and called the station.

In-fact it was several hours later that a break-through was made in the search. The call came through to Antonio's phone from one of the police officers that he had found an outbuilding which was well disguised within a heavily wooded area. The low stone-built building was covered with bushes so that it blended into its surroundings making it virtually invisible unless you were specifically looking for it. It was also quite a way from the location identified by Diago.

Antonio stood back as the officer forced the door lock. He turned to Diago, "You wait here with this officer and Jaime while Fermin and I have a look inside." The chief inspector shone his torch into the dark interior. The building consisted of a single, windowless room. The only furniture consisted of four wooden chairs and a table.

"There doesn't seem to be much of interest in here" Fermin suggested.

Antonio shone the torch around the walls and over the roof and concrete floor, "Perhaps not." But then his attention was drawn to the far wall. "Do you see anything strange about that wall Fermin?" Fermin looked closely.

"Not especially."

"Look closer at the mortar joints," Antonio moved closer to the wall and shone his torch around one particular block. "The stone blocks that make up the thick walls of this building are all firmly cemented in but this one …," he pointed to a block near the floor, "…looks to me as being free." Fermin looked at the block and agreed. "See if you can get me a narrow tool to slip either side of the block. It looks to me as if it can be removed."

Fermin returned from the police car with two flat chisels that he had found in the tool kit. He handed them to Antonio. "Will these do?"

"Perfect. If you work one into the left side of the block I will try to manoeuvre the other one into the right side. Then when I say so if we both pull at the same time we might be able to move the block outwards."

It was actually easier than they had thought. The block was not deep into the wall and came free without much effort. Antonio shone his torch into the gap, "Now isn't that interesting?" The torch had shown up a safe built into the wall, previously hidden from view by the block that the two officers had removed. There were three push button dials in a row on the face of the safe. On each of the outside two, there was a block of twenty-five buttons arranged five by five, each with a letter of the alphabet plus one blank. The middle dial had ten buttons numbered in sequence zero to nine. "Fits the pattern of the code that our friend Sam Crawford deciphered for us."

Carefully Antonio pressed M O O R E into the left-most dial, 6 4 2 1 6 into the middle dial followed by U P T O N into the right-hand dial. Bellow the set of dials was a handle which he tried to turn. Nothing happened. Antonio tried setting the code again, but this time with U P T O N in the left-most dial, 6 4 2 1 6 in the middle dial and M O O R E in the right-hand dial. He turned the handle again and this time the safe door swung open. Peering inside the Chief Inspector could detect bundles of money bound up in elastic bands and what looked like an A4 document holder. Antonio took a pair of gloves from his pocket and carefully removed the bundles of money and the document holder. "We need to go back to headquarters to check these over."

The three police officers and Diago travelled back to the police station. Little was said as they drove along but there was a smile on Antonio's face which clearly conveyed his thought that, at last, they were getting somewhere. Finally turning to Diago he said, "You have been a great help to us, Senior Alvarez, my friend, without your input our investigations were in serious danger of stalling."

In the chief inspector's office Antonio carefully opened the document holder and looked at the contents. There was a list of about twenty or so names together with contact details, a sheet of paper with four, seven-digit numbers and a separate folder with three inset files

"I imagine the names are probably a listing of those individuals that Danny Thompson was blackmailing. That would explain the bundles of cash and why Hernandez would be so keen to get his hands on the list. I have no idea of the significance of the four numbers. The folder, in particular needs more careful investigation."

"All of the people on the list would have motives to arrange for Danny Thompson to be murdered and must therefore be suspects" Fermin suggested. Antonio looked less than convinced.

"But they would have no interest in the murder of police officer Paco Bosque. We are agreed that the two murders are connected and that Paco had information that he had acquired while working undercover in the gang but was unable to pass on to us."

"You are right, of course Chief Inspector." Fermin was always formal when corrected by Antonio.

"This list is of secondary importance to us. It provides a motive, nothing more. We are concentrating on the murder of two men and have reasonable cause to pursue our investigation of Hernandez, if we can find him, through his connection with Frieda Weber." Antonio broke off the conversation as his phone rang.

"Chief Inspector Garcia; this is Inspector González of the Córdoba police force. We have been following your suspect, Freida Weber, and can confirm that she has met a man in La Crispeta, a restaurant near the Mezquita at 8am the past two mornings. What would you like us to do?

"Nothing, I will be with you this evening."

# 24

---

## MATEO

---

"Mateo, I am going to Córdoba. Jaime and Fermin are coming with me. I want you to co-ordinate the checks on the material in the folder that we recovered from the cave in Sacromonte. I have others tracing the names on the list and have asked Edgardo to see if he can find anything to explain the four, seven-digit numbers. But it is the contents of the folder interests me most."

"Yes, sir." Mateo was always respectful of Antonio, particularly when he was being assigned duties. He was actually a bit disappointed not to be following up the Hernandez investigation and going to Córdoba, but at least he was being trusted with the responsibility of leading the checks on the folder contents.

Mateo was the youngest member of Antonio's team; bright, enthusiastic and energetic. He had only been with the police for three years but had picked up first-hand experience in routine investigation within the squad. The folder was currently with the forensic team and Mateo gave them a ring to get an update. After a short delay his call was answered. "I'm afraid that there is nothing much to report Mateo. Only one set of finger prints on the document folder and its contents. We can't match these with anything on the system. The folder has three sub-dividers, each with hand written notes and contact phone numbers. One of these in particular might interest you. It relates to Valdez Kano, the mayor of Casas de Maderas."

"Could be interesting, I'll come over and collect it. Bring the others too"

At the desk outside the forensics lab, Tavares, the person that Mateo had been speaking to on the phone, was waiting. "Here is a photo copy that I made of the contents in the Valdez Kano folder together with the other two."

"Thanks Tavares." Mateo took the material form Tavares and made his way back to the office that he shared with Jaime, Fermin and Edgardo. Jaime and Fermin were on-route to Córdoba with Antonio. Edgardo was at his desk completing an internet search that Antonio had asked for. Mateo cleared a space on his desk and spread out the photocopied contents of the three sub-folders into three separate piles. The top sheet on each carried a separate heading: Valdez Kano, Sierra New Start Builders, Sol de Granada Construction. Mateo spent time reading the contents of each file, making notes as he went. After about one hour he felt that it was time to make contact with Antonio before carrying on. "Chief Inspector, Mateo here. I have been through the material in the Sacromonte folder. There are three files; one on the mayor of the town Casas de Maderas, Valdez Kano, and the other two on construction firms. The Valdez Kano file contains some incriminating evidence, presumably kept as potential blackmail. What do you want me to do?"

The answer came back, "We are just on the outskirts of Córdoba." Antonio thought for a few seconds then continued, "Pay a visit to Casas de Maderas, but don't call on the mayor. We don't want to forewarn him of any investigation that we may wish to pursue. Just have a scout around the town and get back to me."

Mateo looked across at Edgardo who was still busy at his computer screen, "I'm going out Edgardo. Won't be back for a few hours." Edgardo nodded and went on with his search.

Casas de Maderas was fairly typical of the towns just north of Granada. Most of the buildings were cluttered in narrow streets leading from the main square. The centre of the square was dominated by the church and various small cafés were dotted around its edges. Benches were arranged conveniently below Juniper and purple flowered Jacaranda trees. The town hall, with its prominent Spanish and Andalucian flags, faced towards the front entrance to the church. Mateo walked around the square looking up each of the streets as he passed them. None of them were very wide and, due to the random parking, cars and delivery vans moved slowly as they weaved their way along them. A sign post on one of the larger streets indicated, "Urbanización Colina Vista." Mateo returned to his car and followed the route shown on the sign.

The urbanisation Colina Vista was less than a kilometre out of the town but the character of the place was completely different. Here there were rows upon rows of modern two storey terraced villas. Each identical. The charm, variety and appeal of the houses in the centre of Casas de Maderas was completely lacking. Most of them looked unoccupied, probably predominantly holiday homes. A communal pool area lay behind a gated area at the end of one of the streets. Mateo parked his car and got out. The street was deserted, unlike the lively town centre that he had just come from. Everything was very tidy. The development was probably not more than a few years old. At the end of the street was a low barrier and beyond lay fields in the process of being turned into further house developments. Large posters on the other side of the barrier featured the name of a local estate agent, Nuevo Comienzo, and beside this, the builders, Sol de Granada Construction on another. Workmen and surveyors were setting out and laying concrete for the foundations of new homes, while several JCB diggers were altering the shape of the landscape, removing soil and olive trees. Mateo jotted down the phone numbers and addresses and returned to his car.

Mateo drove back to the town square and parked in the first available spot. He looked at the addresses that he had written on his sheet of paper. Nuevo Comienzo were in Calle de Arboles. It was one of the streets leading off from the square. Mateo could see the brightly coloured shop front from where he was standing. He made his way to it and stepped inside. The office was open-plan and its walls were covered in pictures of properties that were for sale. There were three separate desks with computer screens spread out across the floor. A young couple were being attended to at one, a second was unoccupied, but at the third a sales representative was sitting patiently and smiled in Mateo's direction. "How can I help you?"

Mateo spied her name badge and took up the empty seat across the desk from her. "Thank you, Angela. I am interested in buying a property on the Colina Vista urbanisation."

"There are no re-sales on the first phase at present, but we are offering off-plan on the second phase. These will be high quality modern villas with their own pools."

"Who is building the second phase?" Mateo enquired.

"We are selling on behalf of Sol de Granada Construction. Prices range from 200,000 to 250,000 euros depending upon the specification selected. We expect completion of all fifty properties in the next six months. You can see artists impressions on the wall behind me. Can I show you a site plan?"

Mateo hesitated, "These are above my price range. Besides I prefer the look of the first phase properties," and then almost as an aside, "Who built them?"

"These were built by Sierra New Start Builders."

"I'm disappointed that they are not building similar properties on the second phase," Mateo added.

"Sol de Granada Construction have bought all of the land on that phase and I have heard that the third phase planned for next year will also be built by them."

"I wonder why Sierra New Start Builders are out of the picture? Perhaps they have fallen out with the mayor." Mateo tried to make it sound like an off-the-cuff joke. "I suppose that the competition for land around here is fierce and controlled by the town hall."

Angela did not reply at once but then, "You seem very interested in the politics of the development," another pause and finally, "You're not from the newspapers, are you?"

The direct question threw Mateo completely. "No, no." But his response was less than convincing and he immediately thought that his ploy had been spotted.

"I used to work in the finance department of Sierra New Start Builders before I moved here. I'm sorry that we don't have anything on sale from the original development at present but if you would like to leave me your name and contact details, I will let you know if anything comes in." She pushed a pen and blank sheet of paper across to Mateo.

Mateo decided to take a chance and wrote, "Mateo, National Police Granada." She looked at the note for a moment, added a comment and slid the paper back to Mateo. He read it, "Meet me at the café Bella Tapas in the square at 1.00. I can't speak to you here."

Mateo put the paper into his pocket and left. "*Perhaps the gamble has paid off,*" he thought.

From the café Bella Tapas, Mateo sent an e-mail to Antonio to inform him of developments. The short reply came back, "Excellent Mateo. Find out what you can, but don't approach the mayor. If there is any corruption, we will need to involve the Guardia Civil."

Angela entered the café promptly at 1.00 as arranged. "I need to see proof of your identity," she said with some passion. Mateo showed her his warrant card. Angela stared him firmly in the eyes, in an attempt to gauge his reliability. "I need to know that you will treat what I am about to tell you in confidence. I don't want to be associated with this in any way."

Mateo thought for a moment. "I can't make promises, but my Chief Inspector has handled information coming to us in this way discretely in the past, as I'm sure that he would do if he were here now. I will not be taking notes. You can speak freely. Let me get you a coffee."

Angela relaxed a little. "This has bothered me for some time and I am glad now to be saying something about it. As I told you I worked in the finance department of Sierra New Start Builders before my present job. I was in a very junior position but I overheard things, things that I didn't think were right. From what I picked-up, I believe that money had been passed on to the mayor as a sweetener when the company were seeking permission for building on the Colina Vista urbanisation. Also, there were rumours going around the office that the reason that the second phase permissions had gone to Sol de Granada Construction was because they offered the mayor substantially more than our firm had done."

"Thank you, Angela. You have confirmed our suspicions. We have enough evidence to pursue our enquiries without reference to this conversation. You have been most helpful."

With a great deal of relief and her conscience clear, Angela left the café. Mateo phoned Antonio. "Very well-done Mateo. Leave it at that and I will make contact with the Guardia Civil once we complete the Hernandez case. Corruption is a tricky affair to handle and it will be a lengthy and complicated affair to bring to a conclusion. It has to be done by specialists."

"Why do you think that Thomson was treating these contents so secretly?"

"It could be for any number of reasons. We will probably never know, but my guess is that these were prime contacts that he was saving to use later when on his own. Maybe a little nest-egg for his retirement?" Antonio suggested.

# 2 5

---

## EDGARDO

---

Edgardo was sitting at his desk, busy on the internet. This was something that he enjoyed. He didn't particularly like the leg-work associated with police investigations and, besides, this was what he was good at. He had the patience and persistence necessary to complete the on-line searches and he was meticulous with the notes that he kept as the tasks proceeded. Edgardo was a bit overweight, although he would never admit it to himself. Perhaps too much desk work, lack of exercise and the numerous coffees and tostadas had something to do with it. He was absorbed in the present search that Antonio had delegated to him; the four seven-digit numbers that were part of the find at Sacramonte. Mateo was across the office, on his phone to

Antonio. "I'm going out Edgardo. Won't be back for a few hours." Edgardo nodded and headed on with his search.

He had already tried the most obvious possibilities. These were not Spanish or English phone numbers, nor were they sat-nav coordinates. They certainly were not a code. Further coding within the folder would be unnecessary and everything else in the folder was directly readable. Edgardo's current thinking was that the numbers were possibly catalogue references, but which catalogue? A seemingly impossible task. At present he was checking on-line Granada guides to see if he could spot any references using seven-digit numbers. So far, no luck.

The office was stuffy and he decided that he needed a break away from his desk. He went downstairs and out through the car park. Edgardo made his way through the city streets on foot headed for his favourite spot in the city; the Forum building. He particularly liked the Forum building which gave the impression of a flying saucer with a circular, revolving restaurant on top boasting 360degree panoramic views of the city. The walk only took him fifteen minutes. Edgardo entered the building and took the lift to the restaurant floor and stepped out. In the evenings the restaurant was always fully booked, but at mid-day there was room to sit at one of the window tables and order a light snack.

Edgardo took a seat and looked out through the window on the City. The movement of the restaurant was barely noticeable. The whole 360-degree turn would take one-and-three-quarter hours, but he could only spare thirty minutes, tops. From his present position he was looking directly down on the Parque de La Ciencias, the science park. Edgardo ordered a coffee, tostada and a plate of olives. As he waited, he allowed his thoughts to drift. Maybe some inspiration would come to him if he freed up his mind. Edgardo had visited the science park and museum on several occasions with his ten-year-old daughter, Livia. He was keen to foster her interest in science and technology. Casually, he wondered how new ideas and inventions came into being and how inventors made sure that they got the credit for their work. It would be so easy for them to be stolen or copied. "*Patents, that's how it's done*," he thought and then, "*Perhaps I should check that line out as a possibility for the numbers when I get back to the office.*"

On his walk back to the police station Edgardo took the opportunity to call into a small supermarket. His wife worked full-time, and it was his turn today to pick up something for the evening meal and to prepare it. He always took an easy option; pizza was his usual choice. He chose a large Neapolitan, two long bread sticks, a pack of butter and a litre of water, paid for his purchases and went back into the street. At the police station he put the items into the boot of his car and went back up the stairs and into his office.

Edgardo resumed his internet search. He decided to suspend checking the Granada guides. They were a long shot after-all. Perhaps he would have more luck with his present hunch, patent numbers. The format of the numbers did not suggest that they were related to Spanish standards but perhaps they could be British. Danny Thomson was of course originally from London. Edgardo typed "British Patents Office" into his computer and pressed the return key to start the search obtaining several results. All of them referred to the Intellectual Property Office in Wales. He picked up his phone and asked the exchange downstairs to put him through to the number that he had jotted down on his note pad.

A good ten minutes or so passed without any response. "*The lines must be busy,*" he thought to himself but eventually the call came through. Edgardo's English was not perfect but he was more than passably competent having taken the subject at school and continuing his studies through police courses. "This is Edgardo Ortiz. I am an officer in the Granada National Police force. I am following up a lead that we have in an on-going investigation that we are conducting here in Granada."

"Yes Mr. Ortiz, I will connect you through to our enquiries section. Please hold the line." The phone went dead for a few seconds and then some soothing, non-descript music played in the background. Eventually, a new voice came through, "Sorry to have kept you waiting Officer Ortiz, my name is Hugh Jones, how might I help you?"

"I'm not sure if you can, but at present, I am trying to find the significance of four seven-digit numbers, all starting 20..., could these possibly be patent numbers?" He gave over the numbers.

"Well, the format is correct. Give me a bit of time and I will check them out and get back to you."

"Thank you very much." Edgardo put the phone down. There was nothing that he could do now but wait.

The return call came back quicker than Edgardo had expected. "Hugh Jones here Officer Ortiz. I can confirm that the four numbers that you gave me refer to patents taken out in the name of Thomson, a Mr. Daniel Thomson."

"Thank you very much Mr. Jones that is very interesting." Edgardo allowed himself to wallow in a few seconds of personal triumph and then added, "Out of interest, what are these patents about?"

"They all come under the heading of baking utensils." Edgardo was puzzled.

Keen to let Antonio know the outcome as soon as possible, Edgardo phoned the Chief Inspector's mobile. Antonio laughed, "Good work, Edgardo. It seems that Dany Thomson had a softer side to his character. This just confirms what I have learned from Mateo, the material that we uncovered at Sacramonte seems to amount to a personalised retirement package. He would be keeping all this for a later date when he decided that he had had enough of Salón Oscuro.

# 2 6

---

## H E R N A N D E Z

---

At 9pm Antonio, Fermin and Jaime, were shown into Inspector González's office in Córdoba.

"I trust that you had a good journey up from Granada, gentlemen." The inspector indicated that the three police officers should take a seat.

"We made good time, thank you. As you know we are keen to interview Frieda Weber and your information has been very helpful. The reason that we have not asked you to detain her is that we are more interested in the gang leader of Salón Oscuro and we believe that she will lead us to him, if we proceed with caution. The man that she meets in the restaurant near the Mezquita could be Hernandez."

Inspector González smiled, "We are happy to work with our colleagues in Granada and are willing to assist you in any way that we can. I have set up discreet surveillance of Frieda Weber's flat in Calle de Rey Heredia and can confirm that she is there tonight. What are your plans Chief Inspector Garcia?"

"Tomorrow morning the three of us will be in the La Crispeta. Hopefully she will be meeting the man, as usual. Fermin and myself will follow the suspect; we do not want to raise the suspicions of Frieda Weber so we will make his arrest away from the restaurant. Jaime will follow Ms. Webber. I need one of your officers to be with us to identify her."

"That can be arranged Chief Inspector."

"I presume that her flat is rented?" Antonio looked across at Inspector González who nodded, indicating that it was. "Good, in that case I would like you to obtain keys from the landlord so that we may conduct a search of the property in due course. At the moment our priority is to apprehend Hernandez."

———

Although it was only 7am, it was already very warm when the police officers made their way to La Crispeta; Antonio Garcia, Fermin, Jaime and Sebastiano Ortega, an officer from the Córdoba national police. They had already had an early morning meeting in Inspector González's office and all were aware of Antonio's plan. They would sit at one of the tables and order breakfast and wait. Sebastiano

Ortega would indicate to the others Frieda Weber's arrival by getting up and leaving when she took up her seat at her usual table. Although Antonio had been given a good description of Frieda, he was not leaving anything to chance.

————

La Crispeta was a pleasant restaurant. The patio area where the breakfast tables were situated had an open and airy feel. The main restaurant formed one backdrop to the patio area with the other three sides bounded by high masonry walls decorated with flowers and various ceramic pots. Sitting at their table the four men could look out through the narrow front entrance onto the Calle Cardenal Herrero and across to the impressive bell tower leading into the Mezquita gardens. In the centre of the patio there was a small fountain with the water running off towards the front wall through a shallow open channel and into a covered drain, where it was presumably recycled to the fountain pump. Above, the whole area was open, but protection was offered from the sun by brightly coloured awnings, slung between the walls. Small birds flew about the tables picking up scraps from the tables vacated by earlier dinners. In other circumstances the men could have enjoyed the pleasant surroundings, but this particular morning they had more important issues on their minds.

Antonio looked at his watch; it was 8.15am. He glanced in the direction of the entrance to the patio area. Still no sign of Frieda Weber. He turned his head towards

Sebastiano and as he did so the officer lightly tapped the table and got up from his seat. Slowly the inspector turned his head to look back towards the patio entrance. A tall dark-haired woman, well-dressed and sporting a large red hat was making her way towards one of the tables. She wore a short, thin jacket over a brightly coloured summer dress matching the shade of her hat. Frieda Weber sat down at a table near the fountain and waved to one of the waiters to attract his attention. The police officers were not close enough to hear her conversation but it was obvious that she was ordering something from the breakfast menu. The waiter left and Frieda immediately took her phone from her handbag and dialled a number. Antonio was unable pick up any of the brief conversation that she had. All they could do now was wait for Frieda's contact to arrive.

Antonio sat patiently, nervously glancing occasionally at his watch. Fermin and Jaime sipped their coffees slowly, tensely eking out time as best they could without drawing attention to themselves. Time moved on. Still no show from Frieda's contact. It was now 9.15am.

At 9.20am the ring tone of a mobile phone sounded somewhere within the patio making the three officers jump. It was Frieda's phone. She answered it quickly and spoke quietly to the caller. Antonio could not hear the short conversation that took place. Frieda took a note pad and envelope from her pocket, wrote a short note and put it back in her pocket. She then called over the waiter, paid the bill and swiftly got up to leave. Fermin and Jaime looked at Antonio, their question obvious from the expression on their faces. "*What do we do now?*"

"Fermin, pay the bill then go to Frieda's flat, get entry and thoroughly search the place, but be careful to ensure that you leave it looking untouched. Jaime and I will follow Frieda. It looks likely that there has been a change of plans."

The two officers moved quickly following Frieda out of la Crispeta and across Calle Cardenal Herrero, keeping at a discrete distance. Frieda walked through the tower entrance to the Mezquita gardens, made her way briskly across the orange tree courtyard and on towards the public entrance to the Mosque, which was on the right-hand side of the walled enclosure.

Antonio turned to Jaime. "We need to follow, but at the moment I think we are too conspicuous. I will follow Frieda Webber alone into the Mosque and I want you to wait at the exit which is on the left side of the courtyard. It is the only way out. There is no queue this early in the day and the inside is likely to be fairly quiet."

Antonio had been to Córdoba many times before, but he had always been on business and had never been inside the Mezquita. Although his attention was on Frieda Webber, he could not help being taken in by the amazing space that he had just entered. He was immediately captivated by the forest of slender columns laid out in regimented, regular rows. Each column supported the ends of two red-and-white coloured, narrow arches. Above these were a second row of arches mirroring those below them. The semi-circular shape of each arch was formed from blocks of stone, alternating with bricks. The effect of vast space and great height was mesmerising.

In the centre of the mosque was an elaborate Christian Cathedral which pierced through the roof of the Mosque, stretching high into the Córdoba sky. The immensity of the surroundings was spellbinding. But Antonio had no time to spend appreciating this grand splendour. His attention was focused on the movements of Frieda Webber.

Frieda moved purposefully to the rear of the Mezquita, beyond the Christian Cathedral. Antonio followed her. There were very few visitors around so he had to move carefully so as not to raise Frieda's attention. She stopped at the rear corner of the cathedral and took what appeared to be an envelope from her pocket. A vast forest of pillars lay in front of her. As Antonio watched she walked forward along the first row. She lightly touched each one as she passed them. She appeared to be counting them. After six she turned sharp left down the row that she had reached. Moving along this row she continued her counting, finally stopping at number ten. Although he was some way behind, Antonio clearly saw her pick up an envelope which was tightly placed against the base of the column. She quickly put the envelope in her coat pocket, replaced it with the one in her hand and moved off briskly towards the exit. Given the obvious attention to cleanliness in the Mosque the envelope could not have been placed there very long ago and by the same token Antonio surmised that the intended receiver of Frieda's envelope should be along shortly.

The chief inspector took out his phone. "Jaime, Frieda Webber is coming out. I want you to follow her. I will wait in here. I think her contact could be along shortly."

Jaime was standing below one of the orange trees in the courtyard close to the exit shading from the sun. It was not long before Frieda exited, walking smartly towards the tower leading back into Calle Cardenal Herrero. He had to move swiftly to keep up with her. Once out into the street she turned to the right heading back in the direction of her apartment. Frieda crossed over to the other side of Calle Cardenal Herrero, the side with the shops and cafés. As she did so she briefly looked back over her shoulder. An immediate worry overtook Jaime. Had he been spotted or was she just checking the traffic before she crossed? She should now go on to the Calle Encarnation if she was making her way directly to her apartment, but instead she suddenly stopped, as if she had changed her mind, and turned left into Calle Velasques Bosco. Jaime followed.

———

Antonio glanced again at his watch. Twenty minutes had passed and no one had approached the envelope discretely tucked close into the base of the column. He looked around. There was no one in sight. Had he been spotted or was no one coming? The envelope could not lie there much longer without being noticed and cleared by the Mezquita staff. He had to take a decision. Antonio walked up to the column and picked up the envelope. It was not sealed and inside was a note hand written in German. It read:

"Vielen Dank für Ihre Hilfe bei der Beschaffung der Ticket, Karl. Sie waren ein guter Bruder für mich, aber aus Gründen, die ich Ihnen nicht erklären kann, muss ich Spanien. Es gibt keinen Grund für Sie, sich zu engagieren, und daher die List heute Morgen. Ich hätte dich gerne wiedergesehen, bevor ich gehe, aber das ist nicht möglich.

Frieda.

"Something did not add up. An unlikely possibility began to form in Antonio's mind. "Surely not."

Antonio read the note again. His German was a bit rusty but he could just about make it out:

"Thanks for your help in getting the ticket, Karl. You have been a good brother to me but for reasons that I can't explain to you I must leave Spain. There is no reason for you to become involved and hence the subterfuge this morning. I would have liked to have seen you again before I go, but that is not possible.

Frieda."

Antonio dialled his phone. "Jaime, where are you now?"

"I'm outside a leather shop in Calle Velasques Bosco that Frieda has just gone into. I'm waiting on her to come out again."

"Good, but keep her in your sights. I'm going back to her apartment."

Jaime waited patiently for a further five minutes. He suddenly had a feeling that something had gone wrong. Cautiously he pushed the heavy wooden shop door open and stepped inside. It was not a large shop. There were few people inside but Freida was nowhere to be seen. In a panic he went up to one of the assistants asking her if she had seen anyone matching Frieda's description. The assistant pointed towards a second exit which led out into another street. "Yes, she didn't buy anything and left that way a short while ago."

Jaime rushed out through the door that the assistant had indicated. It opened into a narrow lane which was full of tourists milling about. He looked up and down the lane. No sign of Frieda. He had lost her. Nothing for it but to own up to the Antonio that he had blown it. He reluctantly dialled the number but to his surprise he did not get the heated response from the Chief Inspector that he had fully expected, but instead, "I'm at her apartment now and I think that she intends to return here. I don't think she suspects that the Córdoba police know about this place. I also think that she may have spotted you and led you astray so that she could back-track here without giving the place away. I believe that she has made arrangements to leave. If I am correct then she will not waste any time and should turn up here very soon. But, just in case I'm wrong... find her again!"

An hour passed. No show at the apartment from Frieda. Antonio took his phone out of his pocket and called Jaime for the third time. His voice was anxious. "Any sign of her yet?"

"Sorry sir, still nothing. She could have gone anywhere."

Antonio ended the call abruptly, "Keep looking." The anger in his voice was now apparent.

Next, he called Fermin who was waiting in the street outside the apartment. The intention being that he was to warn the Chief Inspector when Frieda came along the street. "Fermin, come in here; I have something very interesting that has occurred to me and I need to discuss with you."

Fermin quickly climbed the stairs and entered the apartment. He was flattered that his boss wanted to discuss the situation with him. "Take a seat Fermin," which he did. Frieda's cat crossed the room and jumped up, settling into his lap. It clearly was looking for some company. Fermin did not mind. He had a cat of his own. The cat purred contentedly as Fermin gently stoked its fur.

"You wanted to discuss something with me, Chief Inspector?"

"Yes, it's just a theory, but I would value your opinion on it."

Fermin glowed inwardly, "Of course sir. How can I help?"

"I think that we are looking for the wrong person. I have reason to believe that Frieda Webber is the real head of Salón Oscuro." He paused to see Fermin's reaction.

"But…"

"I think that Hernandez is just a cover. None of the other members of the gang have actually met him, as far as we know. It's my contention that she pretends to act in his name to get the respect of the gang members. Spain is still a male-oriented society. I don't think that they would take kindly to being led by a woman."

Fermin frowned. "So, you don't think that Hernandez exists then?"

"Oh no, Hernandez exists all right, but he is no threat to us and certainly played no part in the two murders."

Fermin thought for a moment then added, "But we must keep looking for him. If you are correct then he is our lead back to Frieda Webber."

Antonio looked straight into Fermin's eyes. "There is no need. I know exactly where Hernandez is right now."

Fermin looked startled. "You do! But where?"

"He is sitting on your lap."

Fermin jumped up with a start and the cat fell to the floor giving out a shrill yell. It ran across the room towards the door. The silver name tag around its neck clearly in view. It read "Hernandez."

# 2 7

---

## WHERE NOW?

---

Frieda climbed the stairs to the second floor of the public car park in Calle Cairuan. She pressed the button on her car key and the lights on her Mercedes 4x4 flashed on and off. Freida lifted the boot lid. She checked that the small case that she had placed in the boot the night before was still safely there. It was. It was packed with the essentials that she needed for the journey. She shut the boot down again. The loud thump that it made echoed around the concrete walls. The car was tightly parked between two other vehicles making it a squeeze for her to gain entry to the driving seat. It was always a problem at this busy city centre multi-storey car park. Being the closest to the Mezquita it was permanently filled with visitors' vehicles.

She cautiously reversed out of the parking bay, turned the steering wheel sharply, making the tyres squeal, and drove down the ramp to the exit, presented her parking ticket to the automatic machine and drove off into the heavy traffic in Calle Cairuan. Her route took her past the Christian Palace. She glanced over briefly as she passed it by on her right. She made a right turn after the traffic lights into Avenida del Alcazar and then left over the Puente de San Rafael crossing over the river Guadalquivir. She drove onwards towards the N432 leading south-east wards out of the city.

––––––––

Antonio and Fermin waited another hour in the apartment and then the Chief Inspector called Jaime again. "No sir, no sign of her what-so-ever. It's like looking for a needle in a hay stack. The streets and alleys are so full of people."

"Just come back here, Jaime, I think that she may have given us the slip. We need to think what to do now." The three officers sat tensely in the apartment. Antonio finally broke the silence. "I don't think she is coming back here. She may already have left Córdoba, but where would she go? It could be anywhere. There is still the unlikely chance that she might return, so I will ask officer González to have his men keep an eye on this place. I also want him to trace Frieda's brother. They should have a good description of him from the earlier meetings that Frieda had with him. He could be our only link as to her movements. According to the note that I picked up in the Mezquita he bought her a ticket for somewhere. We need to know where it was to and unfortunately, we are short of time. She probably intends to make her get-away as soon as possible."

Antonio stopped for a moment then continued, "We can't just wait to see if the police here in Córdoba can trace her brother, we need to think what else we can do." He took the note from his pocket. This is our only clue. He read it again:

"Thanks for your help in getting the ticket, Karl. You have been a good brother to me but for reasons that I can't explain to you I must leave Spain. There is no reason for you to become involved and hence the subterfuge this morning. I would have liked to have seen you again before I go, but that is not possible.
Frieda."

"He has bought her a ticket; what kind of ticket and where to?"

"It could be any kind of ticket, plane, rail, bus, boat; we have no way of being sure," indicated Jaime.

"We can discount rail and bus. There is no need to pre-book these. It is much more likely to be a plane or boat ticket. Let's suppose she intends to make a clean break back to Germany. Fermin, I want you to make a list of the airports in this area that have direct flights to Germany. We have a good description to give them of Frieda and they will be able to stop her at the gate if she tries to leave that way. Also check ferries to Africa, just in case. We may as well go back to Granada. We can co-ordinate the investigation better from there."

————————

Freida drove on out of the city and along the N432. On either side of the road the fields in the gently undulating plains seemed to be set on fire by the endless rows of scarlet poppies and glowing yellow sunflowers. At the small village of Torres Cabrera, about 15 minutes from the city, she turned off into a petrol station, stopping just short of the pumps. She opened the passenger door and a well-dressed man got in, sat down on the seat beside her and fastened his seat belt. "You did well, Frieda," he laughed, "The note in German was good but the cat ploy was a master stroke. The police will not be looking for me now." The cat had been in the apartment when Frieda had taken it over. At the time it had amused her to name the cat "Hernandez"; a fact that she now deeply regretted. Frieda gave a wry smile but inwardly thought, "You may be off their list but I am now firmly their number one suspect." She pulled off out of the petrol station and continued the drive south-east wards.

# 28

## POLICE HEADQUARTERS, GRANADA

The atmosphere was tense in the common room, just outside the office of Chief Inspector Antonio Ferrer Garcia. The room was used to give briefings to staff involved in a major investigation. Besides Jaime and Fermin there were six other police officers and two others, whose job it was to take notes of the meetings. The ten individuals sat in silence awaiting Antonio's arrival. He had been in his office from early morning. It was now nine o'clock, the scheduled time for the meeting to begin.

Like the others Fermin was waiting for further instructions from his boss. He considered that a lot of his time during police investigations was taken up in this way. At the beginning of a case, when there were leads to follow, there was always plenty to do, but when enquiries dried up and lines of investigation ran cold, inevitably there was little that he could do but wait. He hated these times of inactivity. This Hernandez case seemed to be going nowhere. Perhaps it was time for him to move on and find another career. He was still young enough to make changes. As he waited on Antonio's orders, he reflected on the reason that had led him into joining the police in the first place. He could trace it easily enough to the holiday that he and his wife, Paulina, had at the coastal resort of Santa Pola, twenty minutes by car south of Alicante. The hotel that they had booked into was basic but clean, second row back from the sandy beach, and a ten-minute stroll to the shopping area. The room was on the third floor facing away from the beach but it had a small balcony, just big enough for a table and two chairs. Most of the day the balcony was shaded from the sun by the tall buildings on the opposite side of the narrow street, but that was what they wanted. Parking had been a bit of a night-mare. Fermin had eventually found a spot three blocks away, having first dropped Paulina off at the hotel with the luggage. Fortunately, he did not intend to move the car again before they left. There were no parking restrictions and everything that the town had to offer was close at hand. By the time that he got to the hotel Paulina had already booked in and had the keys to the room.

It was actually Paulina who had been instrumental in the assistance that they had given to the police at that time. Not him. She was by far the more observant, an essential skill for policing that he now doubted that he possessed. They had hired a small motor boat for two hours from an office in the marina. In front of them in the queue were three men who rented a similar boat. The two hours had been idyllic. Flat calm, easy sailing. They had seen nothing of the other boat. It must have turned in the opposite direction to theirs' when it left the marina.

As they were tying up and being helped from the boat by its owner, the other boat returned. There were three on-board. Fermin saw nothing special but back at their hotel Paulina said that she was sure that only two of the original men had returned and that the third was much older than the man that had gone out in the first place. It wasn't significant and maybe she had been mistaken. Later in the week it was reported that a male body had been caught in fishing gear off the coast of Santa Pola. Police were treating the reason for the fully clothed body to be in the water as suspicious and were asking anyone with any information, however trivial to contact them. Paulina thought that they should tell the police about her thoughts on the men in the hired motor boat. Fermin didn't think it relevant but they had gone along to the police in Alicante in any case. The information had proved to be a break through. Apparently the three original men had set out from Santa Pola and the victim had been drugged and pushed over board. The two remaining men had picked up an organised replacement waiting on the small off-shore island of Tabarca and headed back into Santa Pola marina. All this would have gone unnoticed but for Paulina's contribution. The police made the connection and, from the passport details that they had left with the firm which they had to do when they hired the boat, arrests had been made. The police were of course, grateful for the help that they had received and suggested that they should perhaps consider detective work as a career. It was Fermin who followed that up. But it should have been Paulina.

Eventually, the office door opened, Antonio came out and immediately walked over to the pin board on the far wall. The assembly swung round in their chairs and stools to face him. They all knew that in situations like this their chief officer would be direct and to the point, best to keep silent and just listen to what he had to say.

"You know from our briefing meeting last night where we stand with regards to the case against Frieda Webber. We now have reason to suspect that she leads the Salón Oscuro gang, A fact which she has kept from the rest of its members. It is almost certain that it was her that murdered Danny Thomson and our colleague Paco Bosque. How she did so and where she is now, we have, at present, no idea and precious little clues to go on."

He turned to face the assembly. "The police in Córdoba are keeping an eye on her apartment in the off-chance that she may return there. Personally, I doubt it. I think she became aware that she was being followed. Officer González has his men trying to trace the where-abouts of Frieda's brother. He is not directly involved but if he could be traced then he would be able to tell us about the ticket referred to in her note to him. However, no progress on that as yet."

There was a brief pause and Jaime felt able to ask," Don't you think it strange, sir, that no-one came to pick up the note?"

"Not really. I think that her brother knows little of his sister's affairs and genuinely does not want to become involved. Rather proved, I think, by the fact that he simply organised the ticket that she wanted but made no attempt to follow her into the Mezquita where he had left it."

Antonio turned to Fermin. "Do you have the list of airports that have flights to Germany that I asked you to compile?"

"Yes, but it is quite a list." He handed a sheet of A4 paper to Antonio it read:

Girona, Alicante, Barcelona, Valencia, Madrid, Malaga, Seville, Santander, Jerez and Granada.

He continued, "I have circulated her description to the authorities at each of them. I warned them that she would be travelling alone and with a false passport."

"Good work Fermin."

Jaime persisted, "I still think that the note is strange, sir? Don't you think that she was taking quite a chance leaving it there?"

"You have a point, but we must assume that this happened before she realised that she was being followed. She obviously cares for her brother. Her suspicions must have been raised once she left the Mezquita when you followed her out into Calle Cardenal Herrero. You said yourself that she looked round directly at you as she crossed the road and it was after that that she led you to the shop in Calle Velasques Bosco and gave you the slip."

Jaime remained silent. Antonio went on, "We have one other line of inquiry open to us. Manuel Fuentes is in custody. Remember he acted as her fall guy fooling the shop keeper, Diago Alvarez, into thinking he was Hernandez at the cave in Sacramonte when the gang wanted to put the frighteners on him. I think that Fuentes knows more than he is letting on."

————

Antonio looked directly into the eyes of Manuel Fuentes, who was sitting nervously at the other side of the plain plastic table set up in one of the stations interrogation rooms. It was dimly lit but the Chief Inspector could clearly see that Fuentes was nervous. This was when Antonio worked best. "You haven't told us everything, have you Fuentes?" It was more a direct statement than a genuine question.

"I have told you all I can."

"I think not. Let's just listen to the interview we had with you when we first brought you in. Turn on the recording Jaime." The machine gave a sharp click then began.

"Interview commenced at 18.30 hours; those present, Chief Inspector Antonio Ferrer Garcia and Officer Fermin Casillas of the Granada Police Department, Manuel Fuentes and Abogado, Marcos Lopez,"

"You are Manuel Fuentes, a waiter in the beach bar El Arbol Verde in Mojacar?"

"Yes."

"How long have you worked there?"

"I left recently but worked there, part-time, for about three years."

"Why did you leave?"

"I was asked to leave."

"Why?"

"The owner thought that I was taking too much time off."

"You were becoming more deeply involved with the Salón Oscuro gang. Describe to me what you know of the events leading up to the murder of the former leader of the gang, Danny Thomson.

"I can't help you. I was working in the Arbol Verde beach bar in Mojacar that afternoon and evening."

"We will check that out. Let us turn then to the case of police officer Paco Bosque. We have evidence that places you at the scene of the crime around the time of his murder."

"No, I took Paco to the old outbuilding in Calle de las Palomas and then left. Certain Salón Oscuro members suspected that he was connected with the police in some way, probably as an informant, and I thought that the plan was simply to frighten him and to leave him there. He was unaware of our suspicions. We tied him up, but otherwise he was unhurt when I left."

"You say, "We," who else was with you?"

"Frieda Weber."

"Tell me more about Frieda Weber."

"I know very little about her, except that she came originally from Germany, somewhere near Munich and now lives in Córdoba. She joined Salón Oscuro when Hernandez took over."

"The person that we know as the woman in the red hat?"

"How do you know Helen Crawford?"

"We were friends."

"When did you discover that her brother was Dr. Samuel Crawford, a prominent mathematician, specialising in coding?"

"Helen told me soon after we first met. It just came out in general conversation. I thought nothing much about it at the time."

"How did Hernadez find out about Sam Crawford and his skill in coding?"

"I have never met Hernandez so I have no idea, some other member of Salón Oscuro must have passed the information on."

"Tell me what you do know of the mysterious Hernandez."

"Nothing. As far as I know only one person has contact with him."

"And who is that?"

"Frieda Weber."

"My client is not prepared to answer any further questions."

"Then this interview is terminated."

Jaime turned off the recording.

"Now play the second recording Jaime." Jaime did as he was instructed to do.

"Interview with Manuel Fuentes recommenced at

19.05, also present are Chief Inspector Antonio Ferrer Garci, Fermin Casillas and Abogado, Marcos Lopez."

"I don't know who the real Hernandez is. I'm not sure that anyone in Salón Oscuro does, except perhaps one, Frieda Weber. Occasionally, under orders I have pretended to be Hernandez to frighten our clients."

"Go on."

"Hernandez is a dangerous man. I know that he lives alone somewhere in Córdoba and seldom leaves there. When he took over Salón Oscuro it was Frieda Weber who informed us and she became the link between him and our operations in Granada. Any orders from Hernandez are relayed through Frieda Weber. I don't doubt that Hernandez killed Danny Thomson and probably Paco Bosque."

"Someone in Salón Oscuro must have met him when he took over."

"No, Danny Thomson was killed when he was out on his own in the city. Two days later Frieda Weber, turned up at Sacromonte and announced that Hernandez had taken over as leader and that she would be relaying his instructions."

"Where will I find Frieda Weber?"

"I don't know exactly. As I told you earlier, somewhere in Córdoba. I have told you all that I can."

"Interview terminated at 19.20"

Antonio rose from his chair. "This is all very unsatisfactory Fernandez. You know much more than this and it is very much in your own interest that you tell us." He stopped for a moment and then went on pointedly,"

We now know that Frieda Webber is in fact Hernandez, currently boss of Salón Oscuro. I think that you have known this all along." Manuel Fuentes looked generally surprised. "You are wrong Chief Inspector. I know nothing of this and I think that you are mistaken in your belief. Hernandez does exist and is not Freida Webber."

"Yes, you are correct, Fernandez does exist. Fernandez is Frieda Webbers cat."

Fuentes looked bemused. "That surely can't be correct!"

"I can assure you it is. Now do you see why you must tell us all that you know. Currently, we have you down on paper as impersonating Hernandez but it would not be difficult for us to convict you on the evidence so far that you are in fact, Hernandez, and all that that implies." Antonio paused for a moment, as he often did in such situations, allowing the realisation to set in. He went on, "Make no mistake, I will do that if I need to," then got up as if to leave.

"Just a minute…" a pause, and finally, "I might be able to suggest where she is likely to be heading."

# 2 9

## MOVING ON

Freida and her companion travelled on in silence. Thoughts danced around in her head. *"Was she a fool to trust him so easily? Was she just being set-up as the fall to let him escape back to England, back to the east-end of London where he had lived so long with his elder brother, Danny?"* That was where they had met, her and Martin. Martin was the better looking of the brothers and she had fallen for him almost immediately. But Danny was the more intelligent sibling. He was the one who organised and managed the racket that the brothers were running in London. The two men had never really got on from the time they were children. Danny clearly had inherited the family brains and tenacity. He often put his brother down calling him useless and incompetent. Martin's resentment of the situation festered over the years.

When Danny left and moved to Salón Oscuro in Granada, he soon established himself as their leader using all the skills that he had picked up over the years in the east-end. Meanwhile the fortunes of the London gang under Martin quickly fell apart and eventually they disbanded. That was when Frieda and Martin, by now a couple in all respects of the phrase, decided to move out to Spain. Pride had prevented Martin from making peace with his brother and undergoing the indignity of asking him for a job. He moved into a flat in Córdoba while Freida was given the task of making contact with his brother. He had told her that she was to tell Danny that he wanted to make peace with him and to let him as an equal partner in the Granada set up. Salón Oscuro's fortunes were now soaring under Danny Thomson's leadership. The meeting had not gone well. Danny had laughed and told her to tell his brother that he had no place for a loser. He had, however agreed to meet with him to give him some money so that he could survive. It was the most charitable thing he could do he had said with a superior smile on his face. Freida had reported the message back to Martin. He was enraged but agreed with Frieda that he would meet his brother as arranged. Martin travelled to Granada alone. When he returned, he told Freda that the meeting had gone much better than he had expected. Frieda was to join the gang in Granada as a go-between them and a subsidiary group in Córdoba. But there proved to be no such team. Martin had told her that at the meeting his brother had let slip about the funding of the gang and the code, known only to himself, that protected the valuable documents in the cave at Sacramonte. Martin had stressed to his brother that he and Freida were broke and need money. Danny had just laughed at him, as he had done when they were children, repeated that he was useless and refused to give him any money or tell him anything further about the code. Martin begged him to reconsider but Danny just turned and made to leave. At that point he lost control, but had never intended to kill him. He had shot his brother in the back of the neck before he had the chance to leave. It was an impulse and he had immediately regretted his actions. Freida knew that Martin always carried a gun for his own protection, but had never known him to use it.

Initially she was shocked and stunned, but he eventually had convinced her that it was an accident and they had to make the best of the situation. She was to join Salón Oscuro, who would be in complete confusion when his brother's death became known. She was to tell them that a rival gang had taken over in order to fill the void that now existed. The new leader was a man called Hernandez and that she was to be the go-between him and the reformed Salón Oscuro. He had said that it would only be a short-term measure, just until he could access the documents in the cave in Sacramonte. Their future would then be secured and they could return to England to lead a respectable life somewhere in the countryside. The dream had appealed to her and she had agreed to go along with the plan. But, Freida had been completely stunned by the murder of the police officer, Paco Bosque.

She had agreed to keep watch in Calle de las Piedras while Martin put pressure on Bosque while he was being kept in the building over the wall. But he had assured her that it would only be verbal pressure; a minimum of violence. She was completely unaware of the murder until it appeared in the papers. Martin must have shot the police officer and then thrown him over the wall and down into the empty alleyway where he would surely be found. She shuddered at the recollection. This was callous and disturbed and it distressed her greatly. After days of soul-searching she had decided that she was, by now, too implicated in events and decided to keep quiet. But her feelings for Martin and the man that he was becoming had changed.

Without turning her head from the road ahead, Frieda asked, "Where are we going Martin?"

"Granada. I have some unfinished business to complete. It will only be for a couple of days; just until I raise some money and then we will be on our way."

"Granada! Don't you think that's a bit risky?" Frieda was alarmed.

"No, it's the last place that the police will think we will be heading for."

They drove on in silence for another hour or so and then ahead, Freida detected that the cars in front were slowing down. Ahead an officer of the Guardia Civil, dressed in the familiar green uniform, was waving the traffic to slow down. Frieda pressed the brake, a little harder than she meant to and the car jerked as it decelerated. A spasm of panic flowed through her brain. The sudden change of speed roused Martin Thomson from his light slumber. He sat up quickly and looked ahead. "He's only slowing the traffic. The police don't have a description of this car and besides, if they are looking, then it will be for a woman travelling alone and not a couple. I think there must be an accident or some sort around the bend ahead. They passed by the officer who appeared to pay them little attention, seemingly content that his efforts to curb the speed of the approaching traffic was succeeding. Martin's assumption was correct. When they got around the sharp right-hand bend the cause of the problem became clear. A bright yellow Seat Leon was tipped at a 45-degree angle with the nearside tyres deep embedded in the roadside ditch. The four occupants, two boys and two girls, all in their early twenties, stood in their protective yellow safety jackets, close to the nearby hedge and away from the car. They looked shaken but unhurt. "Youngsters driving too fast as usual" Martin ventured. The short queue of cars came to a slow stop. A second police officer with a stop-go board was directing the traffic past the incident. The board indicated, stop. Traffic travelling in the opposite direction were being given priority at that moment. As each car past by the stricken vehicle the occupants strained to get view of what had happened. "People can be such ghouls," commented Martin. "That's a good one coming from you!" Freida thought, but did not say out loud. The flow of cars continued for what seemed an age, but eventually the sign was reversed to go. The short queue moved off cautiously passed the obstruction. Martin glanced over his shoulder through the rear window and then resumed his nap.

They drove on again in silence past the towns of Alcaudete and Alcalá la Real.

About 15miles from the outskirts of Granada Martin Thomson tapped Frieda on the shoulder. "Turn off the main road at the next junction. It leads into the village of Pinos Puente. This is close enough for now. We need to be careful." Frieda did as she was directed. "Pull over to the side, I need to discuss with you how we go forward."

The car was brought to a stop. It was a straight, wide, stretch of road. There were no other vehicles about. It was Martin who broke the silence. "On reflection, I think it would be better if we split up in Granada. I have arranged for you to stay at a safe house in the Albacin while I see to the business that I told you about. You will be perfectly safe there. I suggest that you don't go out. I will contact you when I am ready to leave Granada and I will let you know where we will meet." This was news to Frieda. She felt a passive player in how events were developing. A heavy lorry passed by on the way into the village. The sudden draft caused the car to shake from side to side. Freida felt decidedly uncomfortable.

Frieda was well acquainted with the city streets. She drove carefully along the Grand Via de Colón, keeping pace with the heavy traffic. No need to draw attention to themselves. They passed the Cathedral on the right. The inevitable band of gypsy women were pressing their unwanted attention and sprigs of cut rosemary onto the passing tourists. She turned the car left into Reyes Catolicós, the wide street leading towards the Albacin. "Slow down Frieda and pull over. I want you to get out here." He thrust a piece of paper into her hand. "I'll take the car. Go to this address and I will phone you to arrange when we meet up again." With that he stretched over Frieda and flung her door open. She looked him straight in the face. It was expressionless. Frieda unfastened her seat belt and stepped out onto the pavement. Martin immediately swung himself into the driver's seat and pulled the door shut. He did a quick U-turn in the street and disappeared rapidly back down Reyes Catolicós in the direction that they had come from.

Frieda watched the car disappear. Only then did she become fully aware of the crumpled piece of paper in her hand. She unfolded it. Scrawled in pencil was an address in Cuesta de Gomerez, the street that led tourists from the City up towards the entrance to the Alhambra. She felt decidedly uneasy about the whole situation. Slowly Frieda made her way up the street. It was baking hot and needing to get a bottle of water she stopped outside a small shop displaying newspapers, confectionary and cool drinks in the window. She went inside. The fridge was just inside the door. It was filled with 1 litre bottles of water. The sign above the fridge indicated that these were 1.50 Euros each. Instinctively, Freida glanced over at the newspaper display; tidy piles of El Mundo, El Pais and ABC, amongst others. They all carried similar headlines, an international climate change conference in Madrid and pictures of a Catalan separatist rally in a Barcelona park.

Freida reflected that the owner had overpriced the water and was cashing in on the passing tourist trade. Non the less the bottle felt invitingly cold in her hand and she went up to the counter to pay. She handed a 2 Euro coin to the middle-aged woman behind the counter who handed her back her change. Frieda felt that the woman studied her face for rather longer than seemed normal. The thought passed through her head, "Did she recognise me?" but quickly put the impression to one side. "Perhaps I'm getting a bit paranoid. There is no reason for her to."

Frieda stepped back out of the shop into the street. She looked again at the address on the paper that Martin had given her. From the flat number given, the house was clearly further up the street that she was on. She stood outside the shop for a few minutes before fully making up her mind and then she tore the paper into small pieces. "I think it's time that I made my own decisions," and with that she turned and walked back down to the junction with Reyes Catolicós, turned left and headed purposefully in the direction of the train station by way of the back streets. In the lane San Jerónimo, just opposite the Plaza Universidad, she dropped the torn pieces of paper into a convenient bin. She crossed over the busy Calle Gran Capitn and made her way down the Calle Rector López Argeta and onto the Avenida Severo Ochoa. Freida entered Granada railway station and bought a ticket to Seville. She had half an hour to wait on the next train, so she sat on a seat on the platform, contemplating her next move. The Seville train arrived on time from Almeria. Granada station is a terminal and on-going services stop for five minutes before going back out to complete their journey. The carriage doors opened and a string of passengers descended onto the platform. Frieda stood up, intensely aware that any decision that she was to make now would affect the rest of her life.

———

The following morning the briefing meeting started early. It was 8am. The same staff were assembled in the room as from the previous morning. Antonio entered coming out briskly from his office. "Last night I interviewed Manuel Fuentes. With some persuasion he gave me a little more detail about Frieda Webber. In a casual conversation with her Frieda let drop to Fuentes that she had come over to Spain from England. He didn't think much of this at the time but last night he passed this on to us. It's not much but it does suggest that she might be heading back there rather than to Germany."

He turned to Fermin. "You need to pass this on to your contacts at the airports that they need to be vigilant and pay particular attention to passengers boarding flights to England, as well as Germany." Antonio looked around the assembled staff. They looked disappointed. The expressions on their faces plainly indicating, "*Is that it?*"

He went on. "I know it is not much. We are dealing with scraps. There is no news from the police in Córdoba regarding Frieda Webber's brother." Antonio turned and went back into his office. "Jaime and Fermin, come to my office in one hour. We need to do some further brainstorming."

Antonio looked dejectedly out of his window. How he regretted not having simply arrested Frieda when they had her in their sights in the La Crispeta restaurant in Córdoba. But that opportunity had been spurned. No use in regretting it now. A sudden feeling of helplessness overcame Antonio. The case was slipping away from him and he was filled with guilt that he had not taken the opportunity to arrest Freida Webber when the chance had arisen. His mind was troubled. On deeper reflection he felt that many of the decisions that he had made over the years, both professionally and in his private life had been ill thought through, ultimately ending in regret. Antonio had been married to Andrea. She had lived close to Antonio's family home when they were teenagers. At first, they were just friends but through time they had fallen in love. Initially life with Andrea had been idyllic but he had let his work get in the way. Ultimately his long hours away from home and the constant intrusion into their precious time together had become too much for Andrea. She was intelligent, with a good degree in marketing from the Granada University, and had career ambitions of her own. They had no children, and when the inevitable split up came it was amicable enough, they had just drifted apart. *"If only I had done things differently, perhaps we could have worked things out and still been together."*

Antonio needed out from his office to clear his head. These negative feelings were not helping his concentration on the task in hand. He decided to go to visit his father who lived in an apartment not far from the police station. His father had suffered for years from Alzheimer's and his condition was steadily deteriorating. Antonio's sister, Ana Sofia and her family had moved in with their father to give him the assistance that he required in order to remain in the family home. "*If it wasn't for Anna Sofia, pa would have been institutionalised years ago.*" Antonio's mother had died of cancer when in her early sixties. His reaction at the time was to bury himself in his work to block out the reality of the pain and distress that she was under during her treatment. "*I don't go to see pa often enough.*"

Antonio had a key for the main entrance to the apartment block. He climbed the stairs to the second level and stopped at the front door, the polished nameplate, "Garcia" reflected in light coming in from the landing window. He had a key of course, but felt it inappropriate to just walk straight in. He pressed the buzzer and the door was opened by Ana Sofia. She was delighted to see him and smiled. "Come in Antonio. It's good to see you." They walked through the narrow hallway that led to the main sitting room. Antonio's father was asleep in a chair by the window.

"Don't wake him."

"He has been asleep a while. He should be awake soon. Can I make you a coffee while we wait on him coming around?

"No thanks. I drink too much coffee as it is at work. How are Ernesto and Jadiel?" Ana Sofia's husband, Ernesto worked shifts in the local Carrefour Express supermarket. Jadiel is their son.

"Ernesto's fine thanks. He is at work just now. Jadiel has taken a job in Salobrea, on the coast, working for an estate agent. We only see him briefly at weekends. I think pa is stirring." Then to her father, "Look who has come to visit us."

The old man briefly opened his eyes and gazed towards Antonio but there was no look of recognition. "It's me, pa. How are you feeling?" Still no response. His father shut his eyes again, drifting back into sleep.

"Don't worry Antonio. He is not having one of his better days. Tomorrow will be different." Ana Sofia tried to sound reassuring but Antonio was less than convinced. "I must just see to Carmen's food."

"*Carmen? Oh of course, the cat!*" The irony was not lost on Antonio. People often project personalities onto their pets through the names that they give them. "*Carmen the impetuous gypsy from the Bizet opera.*" Antonio frowned as he again contemplated the lost opportunity in Córdoba.

Antonio's phone rang. "Chief Inspector, I have a woman at the front desk. She says she needs to speak urgently to someone in authority. She would not give her name or state her business."

"Keep her with you. I am coming right back."

————

Back in his office Antonio was deep in thought after his meeting with the woman who needed to speak to him. At 2.30pm in the afternoon the Chief Inspector's desk phone rang. It was an outside line. "I can tell you where Freida Webber will be at 9.00am tomorrow morning." It was a male voice.

# 3 0

## TORRE DE LA VELA

It was a bright, sunny morning. At 8.45am Frieda made her way through the gate to the Alcazaba, the fortress area within the grounds of the Alhambra. She had been up early, unable to sleep the night before, her mind filled with what she was now about to do. Soul searching done, she was content with the decision that she had made and was fully focused on achieving her aim. She knew her future was uncertain, but the die had been cast. The consequences were now out of her hands. It had taken her fifteen minutes to walk from the main entrance and she wanted to be on time. There had been no need to join the long queue of tourists waiting to buy tickets as she had no intention of visiting the Casa Real, the Palace proper.

She was heading for the Torre de la Vela watchtower in the fortress area; no tickets needed for there, and besides it was not her plan to stay long. The narrow stone stairs that climbed up inside the high stone tower were steep, but the few visitors that were around this early still hadn't yet made their way to this part of the complex. There were many points of interest to visit before coming to this end of the complex, so Frieda was able to climb quickly to the top and out onto the open roof terrace. Each of the four edges were protected by low walls. Frieda glanced about her. She was alone. Cautiously she made her way over to the wall that overlooked the Rio Darro and the cluster of buildings in the Albacin, climbing high from the river, on the opposite bank. She glanced over, but swiftly stepped back. A sudden gust of wind almost blew away the red hat that she clutched tightly in her right hand. Heights had never been Frieda's thing and she retreated to a more central part of the flat roof deciding that it would be more comfortable to wait there. Her senses were on high alert and she was acutely conscious of the heavy steps ascending the stair well behind her.

———

Martin Thomson had slept well. The previous evening, he had parked in the underground car park below the Avenida de la Constitution and checked into a nearby hotel. The hotel was classy and expensive, but what did he care, he could afford it. In the afternoon he had gone out. The travel agency that he headed for was in Acera del

Darro, only a fifteen-minute stroll from his hotel. He had made his way through the back streets and into the wide Plaza Bib Rambla, pausing to casually look in some of the shop windows. From there he turned down to the Puerta Real and into the Acera del Darro. He saw that the travel agency was on the right, so he crossed over the busy road, entered the shop and went straight to a glass fronted inner-office area displaying the sign "Servicio de Consultas," the enquiries desk. There had been a short queue, but Martin Thomson was in no hurry. Eventually it was his turn. "I believe that you have the travel tickets that I ordered. My name is Martin Thomson."

The assistant checked. "Ah yes, Mr. Thomson, I have the booking here. One car and driver on Brittany Ferries, Santander to Plymouth one way. Is that correct?"

"Yes, that's correct."

"You have no passengers?" It was a statement designed as a check rather than an actual question.

"That's right, I will be travelling alone." He paid the assistant, jammed the envelope that he was given into his trouser pocket and left the shop in good spirits.

After his four-course meal in the elegant restaurant on the ground floor of his hotel, he had retired to the superior room on the second floor that he had selected based on the advice given to him at the reception desk. He had taken a bottle of best quality Spanish wine up to the room with him, Rioja Alta 890 Gran Reserva 2005. Things were going in his favour and he felt that a small celebration was in order.

Next morning, he had risen early, refreshed and motivated to see things through to their conclusion. The taxi-ride up to the Mirador de San Nicolas had only taken fifteen minutes. He had chatted with the driver. It was the usual kind of conversation that takes place between a taxi driver and his passenger, trivial and general. The plaza was already buzzing with tourists and street merchants displaying souvenirs for sale on small, portable tables. A guitarist walked amid the crowd, filling the place with the tuneful sounds from his skilfully-played instrument.

Martin Thomson walked purposefully to the low wall at the edge of the Mirador de San Nicolas. From there he had a clear and uninterrupted view of the Alhambra on the opposite side of the river. He took a small pair of binoculars from his pocket and trained them on the Torre de la Vela watchtower. He could clearly see Freida standing alone. It was 8.50am.

———

Freida glanced nervously at her watch; 8.55am, only five minutes to go now. She began to shiver uncontrollably as doubts began to flow through her mind, "*Was this really what she wanted?*" The five minutes seemed to Freida to take an age to pass. Then suddenly from below, somewhere in the heart of the city, a loud church bell began to strike. It struck nine times, marking the hour. Freida checked her watch again; the arranged time.

———

From his vantage point on the Mirador de San Nicolas Thomson watched on as the two uniformed police officers came out onto the roof of the watchtower and moved swiftly towards Frieda. Frieda turned to look in their direction as they approached, but remained motionless. Martin Thomson casually tapped the inside pocket of his jacket, checking that his passport and ferry ticket were there. He watched and waited just long enough to see the police officers surround Freida and then, swinging around with a smug smile of satisfaction on his face, made to step away from the low wall.

"Not so fast Martin Thomson, or would you prefer me to call you Hernandez." It was Chief Inspector Antonio Ferrer Garcia's voice. Martin Thomson was startled and his hand went instinctively to his right-hand pocket. "I'll take that if you don't mind." Antonio swiftly took the revolver from Thomson's hand and gave it to one of the officers behind him. Thomson was shocked, his mind and body paralysed by confusion. "I am arresting you for the murder of your brother, Danny Thomson and police Officer Paco Bosque." He turned to Jaime and Fermin. "Put the cuffs on him and take him to the van."

It was a much-relieved Antonio Garcia that stepped up to the low wall of the Mirador. He took his phone from his pocket and, at the same time, raised his right hand high above his head and waved across to the watchtower. "We have him!" The words were said with a great deal of satisfaction and then he added, "Let Frieda Webber know."

# 3 1

Antonio looked around the briefing room at the assembled members of his team. They sat comfortably lounging on the disparate range of chairs and stools randomly spread across the floor. Coffee cups sat on the various small tables that had been brought in from other parts of the building. A large plate of churros took pride of place on one of these near the middle of the room. It was 9am on the morning following the arrest of Martin Thomson.

"It's good to see you all here and a special welcome to officer González, our colleague from the Córdoba police department." All eyes were drawn in the direction of the officer sitting at one of the corner tables. "Alonzo, and

I'm sure he won't me being informal at this get together, proved very helpful in the successful outcome of the Hernandez case."

Alonzo González smiled politely. "It is kind of you to say so Antonio, but the reality is that we were of little help to you."

"On the contrary Alonzo, it was you and your officers that first uncovered Frieda Webber's apartment in Córdoba and subsequently set us on the trail of her unknown visitor at La Crispeta restaurant."

"But we couldn't trace him. We were wrong to assume that he was her brother."

The strain of the investigation now lifted, Antonio added light heartedly, "We were also far off the truth at the point. We thought that Hernandez was Frieda Webber's cat." This raised a polite laugh around the room. "We also wrongly jumped to the conclusion that she was German. It was Fuentes that led us to believe that. He believed it himself. I think that she kept up the pretence to distance herself from other members in the gang. The truth is that she is English. She was born and brought up on the south side of the Thames, around the Elephant and Castle. Freida did a degree in business studies at South Bank University. Our suspicions were raised when we looked more closely at the German note that she produced. On close examination it had the air of having been through an on-line translation system, Google Translate or some such. But the reality is that if she had not come forward to us with the information on Martin Thomson, all be it belatedly, then we would probably have remained in the dark and way off the scent. Fortunately, her conscience must have got the better of her; that and her suspicion that she was being set-up to take the rap for the murders, leading to her handing herself in and coming clean with the information." Antonio took a sip from his coffee cup. "At first, I was suspicious of her statement, but when the later phone call came in telling us of where to find her, things began to tie together."

Another sip of coffee. "Frieda Webber played no part in the murders and was unaware of the actions of Martin Thomson until after the events. Her main shortcoming was that she didn't come forward to us immediately. She was a prominent member of the Salón Oscuro gang and will stand trial on that, of which she fully aware and accepts. In her favour is the fact that she has given us vital information on the working of the gang and I am sure that this will be taken into account."

Antonio stopped and for a moment it looked as if he would say no more. It was Alonzo González that posed the obvious question. "But Antonio, I don't understand how you were able to trace Thomson to the Mirador de San Nicolas to make his arrest?"

"Credit for that has to go to Jaime." Jaime allowed himself to smile faintly. He was pleased to receive the acknowledgement from Antonio in the presence of the assembled work colleagues. "We built up a profile of Martin Thomson from Freida Webber's description of his character. As a kid he had always been in the shadow of his older brother. Throughout his life he had been put down by him and made to feel a failure. The resentment grew in him, initially supressed but finally culminating in the murders that he committed. These were cowardly acts. Look at the facts, two men shot in the back of the neck. But he needed recognition and hence the desire for his evil deeds to be seen. The dumping of Paco's body in the alleyway is a prime example. He wanted his actions to be recognised but to experience the macabre pleasure that these gave him from a distance, unimplicated in the deeds. His blatant set-up of Freida Webber was his eventual downfall. He was not a very clever man. Why ask Frieda to meet him in such a prominent and open place as the Torre de la Vela watchtower in the Alhambra? Given the picture that we had built of his character, it seemed very likely that he would want to witness her arrest, but from a safe distance. He would be unaware that she had decided to come to us and agree to the performance on the watchtower."

Again, he stopped briefly to let the information sink in. Antonio was enjoying this. He went on, "Now this is where Jaime's knowledge of Granada proved pivotal. According to Jaime the most obvious, and perhaps only choice, was from the Mirador de San Nicolas Square. A perfect location, a clear view of the Torre de la Vela and an easy place to mingle in with the tourists who flock there daily to take pictures of the Alhambra. We also had a good description of Thomson from Alonzo's men who had seen him with Freida in the restaurant in Córdoba before we arrived there. I should also congratulate Mateo. His work on the Valdez Kano, Casas de Maderas corruption case is with the Guardia Civil, who report that they are making steady progress and are confident of a positive, eventual result."

Mateo smiled and asked, "Is there any news on Sam Crawford and his wife?"

"I must admit that we have been somewhat distracted recently, but the last that I heard was that he was still at the cave house in Freila and that she was making slow, but steady progress at the Italian convent. I will make fresh contact with him and check. His work on the code was a great help to us in the initial stages of the case."

The room fell silent and no further questions were forth coming so Antonio stood up and lifted his coffee cup indicating that he wanted to close the meeting. "I admit we were lucky, very lucky, but here's to a successful outcome and ultimately, a job well done." They all raised their cardboard coffee cups. Antonio took the last mouthful from his and laid it back down on the table. Unlike the others this one was laced with a modest shot of whisky, Glenmorangie, his favourite. But that was his little secret.

# 3 2

---

## THE LECTURE

---

*"Nemo mortalium omnibus horis sapit."* *"Of mortal men, none is wise at all times."*

Sam Crawford looked out from the podium towards the students and staff seated in the lecture theatre. Each of the one hundred and fifty seats was occupied. He found it hard to believe that just over two years had passed since he had cancelled the lecture that he was to give to the mathematics faculty here at Granada University. But now he was at last ready to give it. The title of the lecture had not changed, "Pattern Recognition as an Aid to Code Breaking" but the content had been amended somewhat. The facilities were superb, a simple click of a switch would start the power-point presentation that he had prepared to assist him during his talk, the microphone was switched on and the lecture theatre acoustics were superb.

Professor Cortes, Head of the Department of Mathematics, had introduced Sam and given a brief resume of his career. Mention had been made of the significant part that Dr. Crawford had played in first decoding the notes of Danny Thomson, former gang leader of Salón Oscuro, and how this had ultimately led to the arrest and conviction of Frieda Weber and Martin Thomson.

Sam took a sip of the water that had been placed beside him and began. "I am delighted to be here with you today to, at last, present this postponed lecture. I have to apologise that it will be given in English as my Spanish is still very limited. I must first thank Professor Cortes for his hospitality at this superb university and for his kind words of introduction. The title of my talk, as you know, is "Pattern Recognition as an Aid to Code Breaking." I think that the title should now also include the phrase "and its limitations." My recent experience has highlighted the part that pure chance plays in real life. Patterns can be deceptive. Things may seem to be progressing along a steady, predefined route, only to be thrown into chaos by some random event. It is also very easy to jump to conclusions too quickly and consequently progress along the wrong track. It is wise to stand back and take time to consider all of the possibilities." Sam made a mental note that, if he were asked back, his next lecture would be on chaos theory.

Sam took a deep breath before continuing. He lightly touched the Dama de Baza statuette on the table beside him and took the opportunity to look out towards the front seats in the lecture theatre. Chief Inspector Antonio Garcia was there as an invited guest, as was Inspector Leandro Manriques, the police officer from Baza, but they were not who he was looking for. In prime position in the very centre of the row, sitting next to his sister Helen, was Carol, his wife. Thoughts and images of the past two years flooded into his mind. "*How well she now looks and how grateful I am for the dedicated care that she had at the convent aiding her recovery.*" Progress had been slow at first, but small, steady, improvements week-by-week, month-by-month, had taken place but Sam realised that there was still quite a way to go. He remembered, in particular, the day that she was well enough for him take her back to the cave house in Freila and the pleasure on her face when she first saw it. Like Sam, she loved the tranquil setting and the views across the valley, the cool interior in the hot summer days and the comforting warmth during the cold winter months. He thought fondly of the summer nights that they had sat out on the balcony, staring up at the stars and how, as her heath improved and her confidence grew, they were able to begin to talk about her disappearance and ordeal in Florence. Slowly, it became apparent as they sat together, that the events had been very much as the Italian police had described. The memories were painful for her to bring to mind at first, but Sam had patiently and tenderly allowed her, day-by-day, to draw out her recollections at a pace she was comfortable with. Sam was also sure, in his own mind, that the Dama de Baza statuette had played at least some small part in the mending process. His thoughts continued to wander, "*She is now ready to return with me to Edinburgh and resume our life together. I am so lucky to have her back.*" Sam looked lovingly towards her, completely oblivious of the others in the lecture theatre. It may only have been five or so seconds, but the assembled guests were aware of the awkward silence that ensued.

Carol beamed a smile back at him and raised her eyebrows. Her message was clear, "*I'm fine, now just get on with the bloomin' lecture.*"

View of the Alhambra and Watch Tower from the Mirador de San Nicolás

For exclusive discounts on Matador titles,
sign up to our occasional newsletter at
troubador.co.uk/bookshop

Lightning Source UK Ltd.
Milton Keynes UK
UKHW020816160921
390679UK00004B/524